"Would yo

Derek picked up the bouquet. "That won't be necessary." He handed her the flowers. "For you."

"Me? But…I can't—"

"Why not? You don't like flowers?"

"I do. But I have tons of flowers at the shop. You don't need to buy me flowers."

He raised a brow. "Really? When was the last time you took fresh flowers home?"

Her cheeks turned a pretty shade of pink. "Um… well—" She shot him a tentative grin. "Sure there's no girlfriend who's going to get jealous?"

"Positive. I'm very much single."

"Well…thank you." The gold flecks in her eyes danced.

Derek moved toward the door and glanced over his shoulder. With a wink, he left. He was enjoying being ordinary Derek Wood, deliveryman.

Kimberly Rose Johnson writes romances that warm the heart and feed the soul. She holds a degree in behavioral science from Northwest University. She lives in the Pacific Northwest with her husband of twenty-four years. Writing is her passion, and she is a member of American Christian Fiction Writers. She enjoys taking long walks with her husband and dog, reading, dark chocolate and time with friends.

Books by Kimberly Rose Johnson

Love Inspired Heartsong Presents

The Christmas Promise
A Romance Rekindled
A Holiday Proposal
A Match for Meghan
A Valentine for Kayla

KIMBERLY ROSE JOHNSON

A Valentine for Kayla

Recycling programs for this product may not exist in your area.

ISBN-13: 978-0-373-48774-5

A Valentine for Kayla

This edition published by arrangement with Love Inspired Books.

www.Harlequin.com

Printed in U.S.A.

"For I know the plans I have for you," declares the Lord, "plans to prosper you and not to harm you, plans to give you hope and a future."
—*Jeremiah* 29:11

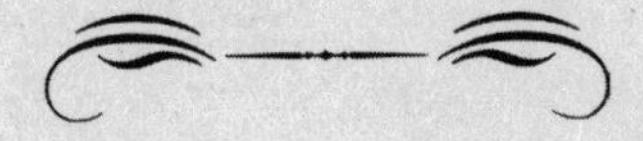

This book is dedicated to my valentine, my husband.
Thanks for your patience and support.

Chapter 1

"I hate Valentine's Day." Kayla Russell secured a flower arrangement in the delivery box, then moved on to the next one in a long line of vases and baskets filled with colorful flowers and greenery. Everywhere she looked there were hearts or cupids to remind her of the dreaded day.

Her best friend and business partner, Jill, shot her *the look*—the one that said *Spare me.* "I'm sure if you had a boyfriend, you'd feel differently."

"Unlikely. Think about it—no matter how you look at it, unless your man is Prince Charming, there's no way he can live up to the hype. The day is one big disappointment."

"I'm glad everyone doesn't feel that way or you and I would be out of business. Have you looked at the orders? I'm going to be working all night just to get everything finished in time for Charlie to deliver tomorrow."

Kayla bit her bottom lip. Flowers and More depended on successful holidays to keep their doors open. Sure, they stocked gifts and music, but the big money came from days like Valentine's. She glanced at the clock. "I wish the UPS guy would get here. He's late, and I needed the cards for the flowers yesterday."

"Use one of the generic cards with our logo. No one will care if there's not a heart on the card."

"I care. I may not like the day, but I want our customers to feel treasured and loved." Kayla fluffed and straightened a bow around a clear vase—perfect.

"For someone who despises the most romantic day of the year, you're quite the romantic." A tiny smile crossed Jill's face before her brow puckered. "This arrangement is cramping my hand."

"Want me to take over?"

Jill's gaze shot to her. "No way. The last time you arranged something, I had to tear it apart and start over."

"I'm not that bad anymore. I've been watching you. I'm sure I've improved." She crumpled a sheet of tissue paper and flung it at Jill.

"Mmm-hmm. You keep telling yourself that, but leave the floral design to me. You stick to making bows and running the store."

The bell on the entrance jingled. "I hope that's UPS." Kayla rushed through the swinging door into the main part of their shop and stopped midstep. That was not their normal UPS guy. This one hummed a familiar worship song and walked with a bounce in his step.

He stopped humming when his eyes rested on hers. "Afternoon." He handed her a small box. "Busy day."

She tore her gaze from his twinkling azure eyes. "Yes, here, too." She raised the box. "Thanks—I've been waiting for these."

"Welcome. Have a good one."

"Come again soon." The last word died on her lips as

she realized how ridiculous she sounded. He'd be back only if she had something shipped UPS. It wasn't as if he were a customer.

He winked and strode his toned body out the door, then hopped into the large brown truck and rumbled down the road.

"Come again soon?" she muttered. He probably thought she was a nutcase, and today that wouldn't be far from the truth. But, oh, he was something, and so polite, too. Kayla mentally ticked through her must-have list of qualities for a husband. Tall, handsome, kind eyes, sings, loves the Lord—

"Earth to Dreamer. Come in, Dreamer." Jill waved a hand in front of her face.

Kayla blinked rapidly and stepped back. "What did I miss?"

"I was going to ask you the same thing. I haven't seen that look on your face since…forever. What gives?"

"The new UPS driver caught my eye, and I made a fool of myself."

"Really? I thought your dream man had to be rich. Last I checked, deliverymen don't rake in money."

"I crossed that requirement off my list last year. I'm not a gold digger and that seemed gold diggerish."

"Maybe there's hope for you yet," Jill called over her shoulder as she pushed through the doorway and into the back room, where all the magic happened, as Jill liked to say.

Kayla carefully sliced open the box and pulled out the Valentine's cards. She hurriedly wrote out messages until her hand demanded she stop. Maybe a coffee break was in order—decaf since it was after five; otherwise, she'd never sleep tonight, no matter how busy her day. Just then the front door swung open and a harried man in a gray suit strode in.

"Is it too late to order a delivery for tomorrow?" He pulled out his wallet and handed her a clipping from a magazine. "My wife wants that." He pointed to the page and rocked back on his heels.

Smart man, or maybe his wife was the smart one. She couldn't be disappointed if he gave her what she asked for.

"I think we can do the job. May I keep this?"

He nodded.

"Thanks. I'll attach it to the order form." She passed him a Valentine's card and pen. "How about you write your wife a message while I ring this up?"

"You saved me. I'm on my way out of town and won't be here to deliver it in person." The man scribbled out something, placed the card in an envelope and slid it across the counter.

"It's our pleasure. I hope your wife enjoys the flowers." She took down the pertinent information, then collected his money. "Have a good one."

"You, too." The man rushed out as fast as he'd arrived.

Kayla took the order to Jill. "I have one more for you." She waved the magazine clipping.

"No! I thought when I said I'd be here all night, you understood I couldn't take any more orders."

"Come on—the guy's going out of town and wants his wife to be remembered. Surely you can accommodate him. Besides, I already told him we could and he's gone. We are a florist, and we can't not take orders. It doesn't work that way."

Jill groaned. "You're killing me. At this rate, I'm going to run out of flowers. Please, no more special orders or someone will be disappointed when their flowers show up the day after Valentine's. Next year we need to hire an additional florist."

Kayla saluted her friend. "I want to help. What can I do?"

Jill set her to doing prep work that a third grader wouldn't have problems with. Not that she was insulted, but lately she'd gotten bored with life at the flower shop. After nearly three years, the ten-hour days were wearing on her. And more than ever she wanted a special someone in her life, but as each year passed, she felt a little less hopeful.

A catalog caught her eye. Maybe she should place an order and have it sent UPS. She'd like to see the new guy again. He was the first man she'd met in a long time who even came close to fulfilling the qualities on her list. She fingered the glossy cover, then shook her head at the idea. She needed to get through tomorrow, and she didn't have time for silly schoolgirl thoughts—no matter how entertaining.

Derek Wood left the little flower shop determined to return soon, even if it meant buying something he didn't need. Not that he was in the market for a girlfriend, especially after that mess with Estelle Rogers, Hollywood's It girl. But he couldn't quench the interest the dark-haired beauty at the flower shop had sparked. Too bad he hadn't met her a few years ago; she would have been perfect for his music video.

But he'd left that life behind. Going on six months now with no paparazzi scoping out his every move. Praise the Lord he used a pseudonym, so they wouldn't trace him to his mother's home in Oak Knoll, Oregon. It was a good thing she'd moved here a couple of years ago, because if he'd been in his hometown, there'd have been no hiding from anyone.

He pulled into the UPS parking lot, locked up, then went inside to clock out. It'd been a long day, but he'd heard stories from other drivers that today was nothing compared with the Christmas season. He shuddered—maybe he'd move on by then. It wasn't as if he needed to work. He'd made plenty of money from his albums.

Derek clocked out, then headed to his F-250 4x4—a present he bought himself after returning from Italy.

He stepped up into his new baby, and with a flip of his wrist, the engine purred to life. He slid it into gear and pulled out of the parking lot. He should've bought flowers for his mom. There was time, though, since Valentine's Day was tomorrow. If Dad were still living, he would have made sure she had the biggest bouquet he could find. Derek sighed at the memory of his father's sudden death last year. His dad's heart condition had gone unnoticed until it was too late.

At least his mom had used the hard lesson with his dad to get her own heart checked out. As it turned out, hers wasn't in great shape, either—a big reason he'd come to town, to be with her.

He absolutely needed to do something for Mom—this would be a tough Valentine's Day for her. And now he had the perfect excuse to go back to the flower shop. Giving her flowers a day early would be unexpected—he liked surprising people.

He detoured through downtown and drove slowly past the shop. A closed sign hung on the door. He frowned and kept going. Maybe he'd have time to stop tomorrow—the gift wouldn't be such a surprise coming on Valentine's Day, but that was fine.

Ten minutes later he swung into his mom's driveway

and sauntered inside. "Mom, I'm home." The house was unusually quiet. He breathed in the faint smell of chicken. Mom had mentioned something about chicken salad. The ticking of the mantel clock filled the silence. Had she gone out with a friend? He lived in the guest cottage out back, but they usually ate dinner together in the main house.

"Mom?" He went into the kitchen and spotted his mother sitting at the kitchen table. "Hey, what's up?"

She turned to face him with a vacant look in her eyes. Was one eye drooping?

His heart hammered, and he rushed to her side. "What's wrong?" He knelt beside her and took her hand.

She blinked and spoke very slowly with semigarbled words.

Something was definitely wrong. "Come on, Mom. I'm taking you to the hospital." It would take an ambulance at least ten minutes to get here. He could have her to the hospital himself in that amount of time. He slid one arm under her legs and the other around her shoulders, then gently hoisted her up and rushed to his pickup as fast as he could without hurting her in the process. "How long have you been like this?" he asked as he buckled her seat belt.

She gave him a blank stare.

He swallowed the lump that had formed in his throat. Mom needed him and he must keep it together. With urgency he'd never known, he drove as fast as he dared. Ten minutes later he parked in the emergency department's lot. "Be right back." He hopped out and rushed inside, then quickly told the check-in lady about his mom and asked for a wheelchair.

The glass doors to the emergency department slid open and his mom wandered in with stooped shoulders. He hurried to her. "I was going to bring you a wheelchair."

She slid her hand into his and gave it a slight squeeze. Her eyes remained vacant, but clearly something was working inside her head. He guided her to a chair and returned to let the triage nurse know his mother was waiting.

Bowing his head and closing his eyes, he prayed. *Lord, You are the great physician. Please take care of my mom.*

"Mrs. Wood." A man wearing green scrubs approached them pushing a wheelchair.

Derek stood to assist his mom into the chair.

"I'm Micah." The man wheeled her forward.

Derek stayed by her side, wishing Micah would walk faster. Not that he was crawling, but picking up the pace would be nice. Surely the sooner his mom received medical treatment, the better her prognosis would be. He stomped down his frustration. Mom slid her hand into his again and held tight. Startled, he looked down. She gave him a half smile. He tried to grin back, but the reality of the situation struck him at that moment—his mom had had a stroke.

Kayla flipped the page of her book. The end of February was notoriously slow. The bells on the shop door jingled. She looked up from the book she was reading and then shot to her feet. Mr. UPS was back, but he wasn't wearing his brown uniform. Instead he had on blue jeans and a long-sleeve black button-up shirt. "Long time no see." He hadn't been back since the day before Valentine's, and she'd spotted another driver on his route.

He grinned. "Yeah. I'm in the market for some flowers."

"You came to the right place. What would you like?"

"Something cheerful."

She stepped around the counter. "We have several nice bouquets and arrangements in the refrigerator, but you're a little late for Valentine's," she teased.

"I wouldn't have been if you'd been open when I stopped back by last week." He winked, then pointed to a purple vase arranged with roses, daisy poms, alstroemerias and asters in varying shades of pink and purple. "I'll take that."

He'd come by? "Great choice. I'm sorry we missed you. I hope your girlfriend will understand."

He opened his mouth to reply just as his cell phone rang. "Excuse me. I need to take this. Hey, Jerry. What's going on?" He walked to the front of the shop and stood facing the street with his back toward her. Too bad she couldn't hear what he was saying. She'd love to be a ladybug on the potted lily plant he stood beside. She always had been too nosy for her own good.

He spun around and walked toward her, a frown marring his perfect face.

She smiled brightly. "By the way, I'm Kayla, co-owner of Flowers and More."

"Derek. It's nice to officially meet you." She placed the vase in a box and stuffed paper around it to keep it from tipping. "Are you working a different route? I noticed someone else has been in the neighborhood."

"Things are up in the air right now." He handed her a fifty.

She punched in the amount on the register, then handed him his change. "Thanks for coming back and not giving up on us."

He picked up the box with both hands. "You have a nice place." Then he left.

She stood openmouthed, staring. "And there he goes once again." He was probably taken—all the good guys were.

"Who goes where again?" Jill carried a bucket filled with carnations to the fridge, slid the door open and set it on the floor inside.

"Remember that new UPS guy?"

"You mean the one who sent you off into la-la land." She snickered. "Sure. What about him?"

"He just left with flowers. I assume they're for his girlfriend."

Jill sobered. "Ah, sweetie. I'm sorry. But as they say, there are more fish in the sea."

"Yeah, well, from where I stand, there's a famine and all the fish swam away looking for better seas."

Jill chuckled as she poured coffee into two mugs and handed Kayla one. "Take a seat with me?"

Kayla followed her friend to the bistro table they kept in the shop for quick breaks and customer consultations. She held the warm ceramic mug between both hands.

"What's going on with you lately? You've been restless and more discontented than usual."

"I know. I guess I'm bored."

Jill bit her bottom lip and stared into her mug. "I was afraid of that. Business is doing well enough. I think we could afford to hire a part-time cashier. That would free you up to pursue—" she raised a shoulder "—whatever it is that is missing and making you unhappy."

Kayla's insides knotted. "I'm not unhappy. Just…not content." She'd put countless hours into this business and took pride in their success. At least they were turning a profit, but that was no longer enough. What *would* be enough?

"I think you need a vacation. This is historically a slow time. Why don't you go someplace sunny and warm?"

"You don't know how nice that sounds." She glanced toward the window and noted raindrops sputtering from the gray sky. "But I don't think now is the time to leave."

"Then when?"

"I don't know. All I know is I can't leave you here by yourself. It's not right."

"Then we'll close the shop for a week. I could use a break, too."

Kayla's eyes widened. "No way. Think about the lost revenue. We can't close for an entire week!"

"Fine—four days, then. We're closed Sundays, anyway, so let's look at the books and see which week was the slowest last year and plan to close from Sunday to Wednesday. What do you say?"

"I'll think about it."

Jill stood up. "Good. Meanwhile, I'll go check out last year's numbers and our bank account. I kind of like the idea of a vacation."

Kayla gulped down the rest of her coffee. Would time off really make things better, or did the problem go deeper than that? The feelings of discontentment were not unfamiliar. She'd had them off and on throughout her life.

Whatever the problem, she needed to figure it out, because vacation or no vacation, she doubted these feelings would go away until she dealt with whatever was causing her to feel dissatisfied.

She stood and glanced over the wall of CDs Jill insisted they carry and was drawn closer by one in particular. "DJ Parker." She'd heard of him. In fact, a few of Jill's friends thought he was amazing, so she'd stocked his latest CD.

Kayla pulled it off the wall display and studied the man on the cover. Wow, he had an uncanny resemblance to Derek, but yet they were nothing alike. Derek was clean-cut and this guy looked like a beatnik.

She moved to put it back, then hesitated and looked a little closer. They could be twins except for the hair and goatee. They both had stunning eyes. She'd always had a thing for eyes, especially blue ones. She shrugged it off and put the CD back on the shelf. She'd have to point it out to Derek the next time he was in—she could only hope there'd be a next time.

Chapter 2

"I'm home," Derek called as he strode into the family room carrying the flowers he'd purchased.

Mom's eyes sparkled. "They-re beau-t'ful." She reached for them and sniffed.

Trying to ignore her broken speech, he handed her the vase. The doctor expected with therapy her speech would return to normal. She'd already had a couple of sessions.

He bent down and placed a kiss on her forehead. "For a beautiful lady. Where should I put them?" He took the flowers from her hand.

She pointed to the coffee table. At least her limbs all worked without a problem and her brain, other than whatever controlled her speech, functioned normally, as far as the doctors could tell. She picked up a pad of paper she'd been using to communicate and handed it to him.

"What's this?" The words covered an entire page.

She blinked. "Read."

"Bossy, bossy. Really, Mom," he teased, and sat on the couch.

The church is looking for a new worship pastor. I mentioned you.

He sucked in a breath and kept on reading, then handed the notepad back. "I wish you hadn't said anything. But now I know why the pastor left me a voice mail suggesting we talk." He sighed. It was time to tell his mom why he'd left his music career. "Mom, being famous isn't all it's cracked up to be."

"Worship pastors…aren't famous."

"I know. The problem is my voice. If I get onstage and sing, anyone who is a fan will recognize it. Then everything will change. I'll be DJ Parker, not Derek Wood. I need to find me again. I need time."

She waved a hand.

"Don't brush this off, Mom. You don't understand what it's like having people follow you everywhere you go and having your every facial expression analyzed." He made air quotes with his fingers. "DJ stepped out alone on a Friday night. Is there trouble in paradise? Could this mean the end for leading lady Estelle Rogers and crooner DJ Parker?" That headline was the beginning of the end for sure.

He didn't regret breaking up with Estelle. She had dated him only to boost her career. The worst part was, that was the same reason he'd originally asked her out. Too bad he'd fallen for her in the process. Aside from being burned by love, he had grown shallow. He didn't like who he'd become.

Mom flipped to the next page on her pad and pointed.

I knew you would say no to singing in church. But music is your life and let's not forget your dream was to be a worship pastor. You just got sidetracked with the fame and fortune. Give your first love a chance. It's not too late.

He doubted that very much. Derek swallowed the lump that had formed. Mom had never been happy about his music career. She'd said God had something else for him, and that he was missing his calling. Maybe she was right. "I'll think about it."

"No! You talk…to him."

"Okay. I'll talk to him, but no promises. I really can't risk anyone hearing my voice and realizing who I am." He shook his head. "You don't understand what it was like living under the paparazzi's microscope."

"You regret your success?" Though her words were slow, they hit the mark.

"No. I loved it. But it changed me, and not for the good. That's the part I didn't like. I need to find me again."

"Good boy. You will." Mom patted his hand and closed her eyes. Clearly it had taken a lot out of her to talk with him. He placed a throw blanket over her, then sauntered into the kitchen. Cooking had never been his thing, but he knew how to use a can opener. They'd received last night's meal from a nice family at the church, but according to the calendar the free food ended yesterday. He was the official cook until his mom felt up to it again.

Derek dug through the cupboards and frowned. It looked as if a trip to the grocery store was in order, or he could go pick up a couple of sandwiches and soup from the deli. The deli won. Mom would never approve of canned soup, so he'd pick up extra for tomorrow, too.

He poked his head into the family room, where she still

slept, then grabbed his keys. He'd be back before she knew he was gone. He jogged to his pickup and headed toward downtown. The dreary day was made a little brighter by the banners that hung from the old-fashioned streetlamps along the sidewalks announcing the Spring Festival at the end of April. Why they didn't wait until May or June, he didn't know. It seemed to him any kind of outdoor activity in this area would get rained out, but what did he know? He'd been there only a short time. The town definitely had pride. From the clean, wide-sweeping sidewalks to the well-kept benches and perfectly manicured City Park. Yes, Oak Knoll was a nice place to live, even if it had rained four out of seven days a week for the past month.

Deli on the Rye was next door to the florist shop. Too bad he hadn't thought of food earlier, but his stomach wasn't growling then. He pulled into a parking spot and hustled inside. He stopped short.

Kayla stood at the counter. She wore a cuddly-looking sweater and an ankle-length black skirt. Her long curly hair cascaded down her back. Was it as soft as it looked? He shook his head, willing the thought away. She turned just then, and her face lit when she spotted him. "Hey there. Twice in the same afternoon."

"Must be my lucky day."

"Mine, too." She shot him a grin.

He sauntered over to her and studied the menu board.

"Did your girlfriend like the flowers?"

"The flowers were for my mom, and she loved them."

"Oh, I thought… Never mind." She grinned. "I'm glad she enjoyed them."

He reached for the order sheet, scanned it, checked off what he wanted on the sandwiches, then turned back to Kayla, who was still waiting for her order. "This place makes the best sandwiches."

"I know. I come here at least once a week."

He stepped up to the counter and placed his order, then sidled up to Kayla again. He glanced toward the window and spotted another banner. "What goes on at the Spring Festival?"

Her face lit. "It's so much fun. The whole town turns out. It's a combination street fair, art fair and farmers' market. People come from all around. There's tons of food and baked goods, too. All the proceeds go to the town beautification fund."

"Here's your sandwich, Kayla." Nick, the owner of Deli on the Rye looked at Derek. "Your order is almost ready. How's your mom doing?"

"Her speech is a problem, but she still gets her point across."

Nick chuckled. "I like your mom. Give her my best. She comes in here once a week for my split-pea soup."

"I didn't know that. Will you change my soup order to split pea?"

"You got it."

Derek turned his attention back to Kayla, who was stuffing her wrapped sandwich into an oversize purse.

She looked up. "What happened to your mom?"

"She had a stroke last week."

"Oh no. I'm so sorry. Do either of you need anything?"

"Thanks, but we're doing okay. I'm a little concerned about going back to work and leaving her alone, though. Her speech was affected by the stroke, and I don't think she could make anyone understand what she needed over the phone. Otherwise, she seems to be fine." He rubbed the back of his neck. "So far my boss has been understanding, but I don't know how many more days I can miss without losing my job." Losing the job wouldn't be a hardship, but he enjoyed making deliveries. It was fun meeting so many people who liked him for himself and not because he was famous.

"Hmm. What's your mom's name? Maybe I know her."

"Helen Wood."

"I don't think we've met. This town feels small and cozy, but it's amazing how many residents I don't know since I'm holed up in the flower shop most days."

"That makes sense."

"If I think of some way to help your mom, is there a way I can reach you?"

He almost spouted out his cell number but stopped. He'd learned after his first album went gold not to give that out. "Tell you what—I have a feeling I'll be in here a lot. Maybe leave a message with Nick, and I'll stop in at your shop."

"Okay. That reminds me. There's something at the flower shop I want to show you."

He raised a brow. "Really? I'm intrigued."

"Good. See you." She flicked him a saucy grin and ambled out.

He turned back to the counter and started when he saw that Nick stood there with his arms crossed over his chest and a wide grin covering his face.

"She likes you."

"Kayla?"

Nick nodded. "She's been coming in here every Friday for the past two years and rarely says a word. I've never seen her talk to anyone the way she just did with you."

Derek tucked the information away to ponder later. Right now he had his eye on dinner.

"I added an extra container of soup for your mom. On the house. You tell her to not be a stranger."

Derek paid and snatched up the bags. "Thanks, man. See you soon." He strode out the door and headed straight for his pickup. Kayla liked him, huh? He wasn't sure what to do with that bit of knowledge. Of course, Nick could be wrong. Not that it mattered, since he wasn't in the market for a girlfriend. Right now he needed to focus on getting his mom well and figuring out what to do with the rest of his life.

"You remember Derek?"

"The UPS guy, right?"

"Yes, well, his mother had a stroke last week. She's doing okay, but he said her speech has been affected. He's afraid to leave her alone for any length of time, and I thought maybe she could hang out here with us."

Jill looked up with wide eyes. "I don't know. I'm not great around old people. Especially sick ones."

"She's not sick and she's not old. Think of her as your mother. Surely you'd want someone to keep your mom company if she'd had a stroke. Her name is Helen Wood. Maybe you know her."

"Oh! Why didn't you say so? Of course I know Helen. She's an absolute sweetheart. I had no idea she had a son. I'd heard she had a stroke but didn't connect her with Derek. You'd think she would have mentioned him." She hung her head, and her cheeks reddened. "You're right—she isn't old. She's good friends with my mom. And guess what else. She's an accountant."

"You're kidding."

"Nope. My mom said she still has her faculties. Maybe she would be willing to look at our books while she's hanging out here and give us some advice on how to boost profits. I really want this place to do exceptional."

Kayla pressed her lips together. Jill was needlessly worrying since their profits were decent, but there was no harm in trying to improve. "We'll need to talk with Derek and find out if his mom is up to it, but I see no harm in asking."

Kayla busied herself with her preopening routine—dusting, sweeping, mopping when needed and washing fingerprints off all the windows.

Time flew, and an hour later she flipped the closed sign to open and propped the door wide with a wagon filled with flowers. These sunny days were a rare treat she intended to take advantage of. She smiled at a passerby, then went inside.

Kayla grabbed yesterday's money bag from the safe and slipped it into her large purse. "Off to the bank. Be back soon." She headed out the door, made a left, passed Deli on the Rye and kept going.

She spotted a UPS truck parked ahead and picked up her pace. Maybe it was Derek. Her heart rate quickened. An unfamiliar man wearing the standard brown uniform stepped out of the phone store across the street and jogged across the two-lane road. Deflated, she slowed down. She'd hoped it was him.

Oh well—she could simply leave a message with Nick at the deli as Derek had suggested. She doubled back, and reaching for the door to Deli on the Rye, she lost her balance as it suddenly swung inward. She fell forward, and steady hands grasped her shoulders.

"Hello, Kayla. We meet again. Are you all right?"

Kayla blinked and nodded. "Kismet. I was going to leave a message for you."

He grinned. "Really?"

"Yes. It's about your mom. Jill, my business partner, and I would like to help. We were thinking she could hang out at the shop some days so you could go back to work."

He shook his head. "That's not necessary."

"Of course not, but that's what friends do. They help each other."

"Hmm. I didn't realize we were friends." He winked.

"In that case, let me talk with my mom and see what she thinks. Maybe she'd be up to it for part of the day." He pulled his phone out of his pocket. "If you'll give me your number, I'll call you."

She rattled off her cell number and nearly floated to the bank, then back to the florist shop.

"Are you okay?" Jill's tone sounded anxious in the otherwise peaceful shop.

"Perfect—Derek has my number."

Jill giggled. "I think he had your *number* the minute he stepped in here."

Kayla stuck her tongue out, then joined her friend in a gigglefest. She wrapped an arm around her stomach and tried to slow her breathing and stop laughing. "Sorry. I didn't sleep well last night, and you know how I am when I'm tired."

Jill nodded. "Exactly like me. I didn't sleep, either. All I could think about was taking a vacation." She waggled her brows. "I was considering Palm Springs. What do you think? I already looked at our orders, and there's nothing for the next seven days. We could close up the shop all week or just until Wednesday."

"I don't know if closing up is such a great idea. Especially if you're worried about profits. Even if we hold a sale to get rid of the cut flowers in the fridge, we'd take a hit. We need to be open to make money. What about your mom? Do you think she'd come in and run the place for a few days? Or better yet, we take separate vacations and leave the shop open."

Jill crossed her arms and leaned against the counter. "Actually, that's a good idea. I'll see if my mom would cover for you, but what about me? We'd have to find someone who can do what I do."

"What about hiring Ashley temporarily?"

"She's still in high school."

"But she's eighteen and graduates this May. What if you plan your trip for this summer? That would give you more time to work with her and become confident in her skill."

Jill broke into a smile. "I'll talk to her after school."

Footsteps sounded behind her. "Excuse me."

Derek!

Chapter 3

Derek stood in the flower shop's entrance, his gaze on Kayla. Her cocoa-colored hair cascaded down her back in loose ringlets.

Her face lit in a smile as she stepped toward him. "This is a surprise."

"I wanted to say thanks for inviting my mom to hang out here, but I don't think it will work." Although the offer was meant to be kind, he could see nothing kind about asking his mother to sit in a public place for several hours.

The smile slid from her face. "I'm sorry to hear that. I wish her a speedy recovery. If there's anything at all we can do, please let us know."

He nodded. What was it about Kayla that made him regret turning her down? Maybe it was the sincerity with which she made the offer—no strings attached. She was so different from the kind of women he usually dated. Not that he was thinking of dating Kayla. His time was consumed with taking care of his mother right now.

The other woman stepped forward and held out her hand. "I'm Jill. Your mom and mine are friends. I think she's planning to invite Helen over, so maybe that will work better for her needs."

"That's a good idea. She needs to be around her friends," Derek said.

Jill reached for the phone. "Good. I'll let my mom know. I think she was planning to stop by and visit Helen today. Maybe the two of them already worked things out."

He grinned. "That wouldn't surprise me. Mom doesn't fill me in on all the details of her life." He looked around the store. The space was light and uncluttered, but it still contained a lot of merchandise he hadn't noticed the first couple of times he'd dropped in. One side of the business held potted plants and fresh flowers, while the other side was stocked with gift-type items—knickknacks, cards, books, teas and coffees, and candies. His gaze stopped at the corner wall. "You carry music."

Kayla grinned. "Yes, in fact, there's a CD I've wanted to show you." She breezed by him.

He followed and nearly stopped breathing when he spotted the CD she reached for—his latest-and-greatest collection.

"Check this out. You could be long-lost brothers. You have the exact same eyes." She studied his face and then looked back at the CD jacket. "It's uncanny how much you look alike. Of course, this can't be you. Why would a famous singer be living in this small town and working for UPS?" With a shrug, she placed it back on the shelf.

He swallowed the lump in his throat and willed his thudding heart to slow, unable to believe she didn't push the issue. He blew out a sigh. "Yeah. Small world."

"I was going to have a cup of coffee. Care to join me?"

She motioned toward a coffeemaker placed near a bistro table.

"Umm, yeah. Sure." Could he sound any more Neanderthal? He shook his head.

"Something wrong?" Kayla poured the rich-smelling brew into a white mug.

"Nope. You ever listen to DJ Parker?"

"Not yet." She handed him the mug and poured one for herself, then tossed a couple sugar packs on the table, along with a few creamers. "I thought about looking him up on Amazon and taking a listen, though."

"Why don't you?" What was he doing? Talk about self-sabotage.

Her face brightened. "Sure. I'll grab my laptop." She stood and rushed through the swinging doors.

He buried his head in his hands. He was playing with fire and likely to get scorched. Call it his ego, but he wanted her to like his singing.

Kayla came back and set the computer on the table between them. A moment later a sample of his least favorite song from his latest-and-greatest album piped into the room.

He held his breath, not taking his eyes from her face. "What do you think?" Why did her answer feel like life or death?

"I'm not sure yet." She clicked on the next song and a smile tipped her lips. Such soft-looking lips. "I like this one. The melody makes more sense than the first one." Her gaze slammed into his, and she caught her breath.

He saw confusion, and a spark of interest resonated in her chocolate-colored eyes. He looked away, unwilling to explore the feelings her look brought on.

Kayla closed the laptop. "I see why Jill ordered his CD.

He has a nice sound." Her words came out rushed as she pushed back in the chair.

He reached out and caught her hand. "Can we visit a bit longer?" He was encouraging her interest knowing it was a bad idea for both of them. Kayla was a sweet, caring woman who deserved more than a fraud like him, but he couldn't help being drawn to her innocence and kindness. Plus there was something about her that made him feel good inside when he was with her.

"I suppose I could sit a few more minutes." She motioned to his mug with a shaky hand. "You don't like coffee?"

"I'm more of a mocha kind of guy." He took a sip and did his best to keep a straight face. "This isn't bad, though. Thanks."

She stared into her coffee.

"Nickel for your thoughts."

"You'd be overpaying." She shot him a smirk, then rose. "I should get to work."

He pushed back and stood slowly. "And I should check on my mom. But before I go, I'd like to buy a bouquet."

"Sure." She headed to the refrigerator. "What kind of flowers would you like, or do you prefer one of the premade arrangements?"

"How about you pick out your favorite?" He enjoyed the look of surprise in her eyes before she quickly veiled it.

"In that case…" She pulled a glass vase filled with light orange roses and small purple flowers from the glass refrigerator. "I love how different this design is from the rest. I'm sure your mom will appreciate its uniqueness."

"Great." He pulled out his wallet and paid.

"Would you like me to pack it in a box so it won't tip on your way home?"

He picked up the vase. "That won't be necessary. These

won't be going home with me." He handed her the flowers. "For you."

"Me? But…I can't—"

"Why not? You don't like flowers?"

"Of course I do. But I have tons of blooms. You don't need to buy me flowers."

He raised a brow. "Really? When was the last time you took fresh flowers home or someone sent you flowers?"

Her cheeks turned a pretty shade of pink. "Umm… well—"

"Please accept them."

"Thanks. You sure there's no girlfriend that's going to get jealous?" She shot him a tentative grin.

"Positive. I'm very much single and would very much like to take you to dinner. How about it?"

"Sounds like fun." The gold flecks in her eyes danced.

"Great. You free tomorrow night?"

She nodded.

He suggested a time and typed her address into his smartphone. "I'll see you tomorrow night." He moved toward the door and glanced over his shoulder and met her eyes. With a wink, he left. He was enjoying being ordinary Derek Wood, deliveryman.

Kayla wrapped her arms around her middle and watched as Derek sauntered out of view. For the first time she seriously considered tearing up her husband-requirements list. Derek probably met nearly all of them, anyway.

"Eeek!" Jill bounded through the swinging door. "I can't believe he asked you out and you said yes! What about your list?"

Kayla pressed her lips together to keep from laughing, but a giggle escaped. "I'm sure he meets most of my must-haves. Besides, I couldn't say no to a man who cares so much about his mother." She motioned to the vase on the counter. "He bought me flowers."

"I heard." A dreamy look covered Jill's face. "He has to be the most romantic man I know. I'm glad you said yes."

"Me, too." She looked toward the front of the store as if he might suddenly appear. With a sigh, she faced Jill. "What's on the agenda for today?"

Her friend rolled her eyes. "In a moment of insanity this morning, I agreed to do a wedding for this Saturday evening."

"No way. But that's only two days away!"

Jill shrugged. "She was desperate, and I felt sorry for her. It's not that big a deal, but I'll need your help making the bows. You're the bow-making expert around here."

"Sure." She followed Jill into the workroom happy she could help in a tangible way. "How many do you need?"

Jill slid the order form across the counter. "A lot."

"Oh, boy. You weren't kidding. Are we only doing bows, or flowers, too?" Kayla couldn't believe the number of bows she needed to make.

"There will be flowers on the candelabras and on the cake. The bride is allergic to flowers and wants to have a bow bouquet for herself and her bridesmaids."

"Doesn't she realize those are only for the rehearsal?"

"Believe me," Jill said, "I tried to convince her to use flowers, but she is one stubborn bride."

"Okay. May I include some silk flowers?"

"How about you make it, and I'll run it by her when she stops in this afternoon? If she hates it, we can change it."

"You mean *I* can change it." No matter. Kayla would make a bouquet so beautiful no bride in her right mind would consider turning it down.

"It's an evening wedding and her colors are silver, white and black."

"Got it." She set to work. "Will you need me to help with the setup?"

"Not this time. Charlie is going to give me a hand. I'm glad we hired him. Our customers really like him, too."

Kayla grinned. "They should—he's a big teddy bear." Charlie was built like a linebacker but had a gentle spirit. She rarely had occasion to see him since he came and went from the workroom to the van parked in the alley behind the store, but when she did, he was always very kind. In fact, she half wondered if Jill had a thing for him, but she wouldn't go there—at least not today.

"When you're done with that bouquet, go ahead and start on the bridesmaids'. I'd like to have them finished by four. She's supposed to stop by about then to see what we've done."

"Will do. It's a good thing we decided not to close up shop and take a vacation or we'd have missed out on this wedding." Always the glass-half-full kind of person, Kayla had to point out the silver lining.

Jill nodded. "But it kind of irks me that she waited until two days before the wedding to think about booking a florist. Who does that?"

"Someone allergic to flowers?" Kayla raised a brow.

"That's what she said, too. Her soon-to-be mother-in-law finally convinced her to go with the bows, and flowers on the cake and the candelabra arrangements. Can you believe we were the only florist she could find?"

"Uh, yeah. I'm surprised you agreed to do the job on such short notice. It makes us look desperate."

"Well, I'm as much a romantic as you, and I wanted her to have a beautiful wedding. I'd have consulted with you, but she stopped in while you were at the bank this morning."

"Now I understand. It's fine. We're doing our good deed

for the week." She shot Jill a grin and reached for a spool of sheer silver organza ribbon. In no time she had a rhythm going and soon the bouquet looked perfect. She'd tucked a few tiny silk flowers in for texture. "What do you think?"

"Nice. I like the variety of ribbon you used. It adds depth and great texture. Who knows? Maybe this will become the new rage."

"Doubtful." Kayla moved on to the bridesmaids' bouquets. If she ever married, she would have tons of flowers and zero bows. She had to give this bride credit for her color choice, though. Maybe she'd even use those colors herself someday. Her thumb caught on the point of the wire. "Ouch!"

"Be careful. I don't want blood on the ribbon. It's expensive."

"I know, I know." Enough daydreaming about a wedding that probably would never happen. Then again... A smile kissed her lips as Derek's image danced across her mind.

Chapter 4

Kayla stood before her bedroom mirror. The List hung beside it. She'd looked at it so often through the years that it had grown thin and tattered. She'd framed it and hung it in a place where she'd see it often to remind her not to settle like her mom.

No way would she get stuck in a marriage like her parents had endured. Not that Mom and Dad were unhappy all the time, but she could tell they were missing that spark. They behaved more like acquaintances than people in love. She wanted that special something that came along only once in a lifetime.

Her husband must love the Lord, love her, be honest, trustworthy, fun, a hard worker and a good listener, be dedicated to her, respect her, treat her like a princess, be committed to family, not take himself too seriously and be easy to look at. Blue eyes—she'd always had a thing for blue eyes. And he had to be able to say "I'm sorry." Her dad had been incapable of uttering those words.

The other things on her list weren't deal breakers, but she'd love it if he could play guitar and sing and be willing to take her on a honeymoon in Venice. She'd always dreamed of being serenaded on a gondola by her husband. She sighed and returned her focus to the task at hand—finding the perfect outfit for her date.

She dressed in a pair of designer jeans she'd splurged on and a white T-shirt, then added a red blazer.

Not completely sure about the outfit, she held up a dark gray midi skirt that hit just above her ankles. She was going for flirty, but with the blazer it came off looking more like business wear. She glanced at the clock on her bedside table. She needed to make a decision. She tossed the skirt on her queen-size bed and held up a tailored white blouse. "Ugh. Now I look like waitstaff."

Why was it so hard to figure out what to wear? Good thing she didn't date often or her room would look as if a cyclone had blown through. She tossed the blouse on the bed, then put a floral infinity scarf over her head and arranged it around her neck. "Perfect."

The doorbell pealed. "Be right there!" She grabbed her boots on the run and zipped them up over her jeans before pulling the door open.

Derek grinned. "You look great."

Before she could stop herself, she gave him a once-over from head to toe. He'd chosen jeans, too. *Whew.* And a black button-up shirt that fit just right. "So do you."

"Thanks. You ready?"

"Yep." She grabbed her purse on the way out the door and locked up. "I'm starved." She glanced into his smiling face. "I probably shouldn't have admitted that."

"Not at all. I happen to be ravenous myself." He pulled open the passenger door to his 4x4 and helped her step up.

A new-car smell engulfed her, and she settled into the

seat. For a delivery guy, he must make good money to afford a rig like this. Not that money mattered—she was simply surprised.

Derek gently shut the door and hopped in on his side a moment later.

Her heart pitter-pattered. Now that she was here, she didn't know what to say or how to act. It had been a *very* long time since she'd gone on a date. And this wasn't just any date—he could be *the one*.

He backed out of her driveway and pointed the truck toward downtown. "I probably shouldn't admit this, but I asked my mom about a good place to have dinner. She recommended Jim's Steak House on Third Street."

"I've never been, but I've heard it's great. How's your mom doing?"

"Improving every day. Her speech is still slow, but the words are clearer than they were right after her stroke. The speech therapist is impressed." His chin lifted slightly.

"That's wonderful." She studied his profile as he focused on the road. The resemblance between Derek and the singer DJ was uncanny. She'd downloaded a bunch of his songs and had been listening to them all day. The man sang with such conviction; she was addicted. "Do you sing?"

He whipped his head toward her, then back toward the road. "Where did that come from?"

"Just curious."

He pulled into a parking lot. "I can sing. Why do you ask?"

Should she tell him about her list? Definitely not. "Guess I'm nosy." She hopped out of the truck before he could open her door.

"What about you? Do you sing?" He asked as they walked side by side into the steak house.

"I can carry a tune." He didn't need to know she'd

placed in every singing competition she'd ever entered—it was embarrassing to share that kind of thing. The talent shows on television were too terrifying to consider participating in, and all but one of the competitions she'd been in seemed insignificant by comparison. She shook her head at the direction of her thoughts. Here she was with a gorgeous, sweet man, and all she could think about was her list.

Derek left her for a moment to give his name to the hostess and a few minutes later she called them and guided them through the dimly lit space. Every table sat in its own alcove, making the setting very romantic. A flickering fire in the oversize stone fireplace against the far wall created dancing shadows. Glass tinkled and soft music filtered through the speakers.

"Will this work?" the hostess asked.

"It's fine. Thanks," Derek said as he sat and accepted the one-sided paper menus from the hostess before she walked away. "They don't have much to choose from."

"That means what they do have will be extra delicious since they aren't trying to make too many things."

"That's a nice way to look at it." He laid the paper on the table. "Tell me about yourself, Kayla. Every time I see you, you surprise me."

She blinked rapidly. "Really? How so?"

"For example, the first time we met, you seemed… frazzled and a little irritated."

Her cheeks heated. "Oh. You're way more observant than I realized. I *was* frazzled and irritated. It was the day before my least favorite day of the year, and I was anxious for your delivery."

"Least favorite day? You mean you don't like Valentine's Day? Why?"

She rolled her eyes. "Where do I start?"

* * *

Derek sat back and crossed his legs at his ankles. He'd definitely touched on a hot topic with Kayla. He'd never seen her so animated.

"I know it seems crazy for someone who owns a florist shop to hate one of our busiest holidays, but really, why do we have to have a special day to show someone we love them? Shouldn't we be doing that all the time? And what about those people who don't have a special someone? It's depressing! On top of that, expectations are so high for a day like Valentine's that we set ourselves up for disappointment."

"Wait a minute. You keep saying *we*. Did you have a bad Valentine's experience?"

She reached for the water goblet the hostess had delivered during her tirade. "Let's just say I've been disappointed."

"Okay. Why else don't you like the day?" He couldn't help asking. Her sparkling eyes as she spoke were fun to watch, as was the animation on her face.

"It's a holiday designed to keep card stores, chocolate companies and florists in business. It's consumerism at its finest."

"Okay, but it encourages people to be selfless and give to someone else. It's not like they are going out and buying themselves things. People are trying to show love."

She bit her bottom lip, and stillness came over her as she rested her hands on the table. "Yes, but what about those men or women who don't care about the day? Their spouse or significant other feels hurt every year when the holiday goes by unacknowledged. My dad never did anything for my mom on Valentine's, and I felt horrible for her every year. Mom put on a brave front and said they didn't 'do' the silly holiday, but I saw the hopeful look in her eyes every year. I know she was wishing for flowers just once. Even though they didn't 'celebrate' Valentine's, Mom always cooked an extra-special meal. My dad didn't have a clue, and it really hurt to watch."

"Where's he now?"

"He died several years ago."

He reached across the table and rested his hand on hers and waited until she raised her gaze to meet his. "I'm sorry. What about your mom?"

Though sadness filled her eyes, a smile touched her lips. "Every February she packs up and goes someplace sunny. This year she went to Florida. The rest of the year she lives with me. When Dad died, she sold the house and moved in."

"How's that working out?"

"It's fine. If it weren't for Valentine's Day, February would be my favorite month of the year."

He chuckled and moved his hand away. "Because you have the house to yourself?"

She nodded.

Their server appeared seemingly out of nowhere and took their orders.

"What about you? I've been doing all the talking." She took a sip of water.

"What do you want to know?"

"Everything. Why are you living with your mom, for starters?"

He cringed. "I recently made a rather large change in my life and decided the best place to work things out in my head was at my mom's place. I was living in the guest cottage behind her house, but after her stroke, I moved into the guestroom."

She leaned in. "Oh, so how are you doing? Have you found any answers?"

"Not yet. Her stroke put my thinking time on hold." Besides, the longer he spent in Oak Knoll, the more he wanted to stick around. Maybe it was time to give Pastor Miller a call about the worship leader position. He'd been here long enough to know who liked him for himself and not because he was famous. The anonymity he'd experienced over the past month had been a godsend, but it was time to face who he was, and his music was a huge part of his identity.

"How do you like working for UPS?"

"It was great."

"Was?"

"Yeah, I turned in my notice. I want to be there for my mom."

A frown marred her beautiful face.

"What did I say wrong?"

"Nothing. I feel bad for your situation. What are you going to do?"

"Time will tell. I have money put away, so that's not an issue." She truly seemed concerned for his situation, which endeared her to him. Not many people over the past several years cared much about him. They cared only about what he could do for them.

Kayla was a breath of fresh air. *Hmm, "Breath of Fresh Air" would make a good song title.*

She grinned wide. "You went somewhere for a minute. Glad you decided to rejoin me."

He chuckled. The woman certainly demanded his whole attention, but he didn't mind delivering. Their food arrived, and he breathed deeply the scent of baked potato and steak. "Do you mind if I bless the food?"

She bowed her head.

He offered a quick prayer.

"This looks so good. I haven't had a steak in years." She reached for her knife and dug in.

He enjoyed watching her a moment too long, and her hand froze midair.

"Do I have something on my face?" She put her fork down and reached for her napkin.

"You're fine. I didn't mean to stare, but it was fun watching you enjoy the steak. I eat these so often I forget what a treat it is to most people."

"You're right. It is a treat." She waved a hand. "I'm not going to ask why you eat steak so often, but if you care to share..." She raised a brow.

He cut into the meat and stuffed a piece into his mouth in reply.

Kayla chuckled. "I like you, Derek Wood. You're still a mystery, but I like you. Thanks for this."

He winked and forked another bite into his mouth.

The evening flew by with good conversation and way too much food. Before he realized it, the waitstaff was quietly preparing the restaurant to close. He checked the time on his phone. Where had the evening gone? "I think we'd better go." He paid and left a very generous tip for monopolizing the table the entire evening.

Kayla's eyes widened at the bill he'd dropped on the table, but to her credit she didn't say a word.

They stepped out into the clear evening. Kayla slipped her arm through his. "It's gorgeous tonight."

"Want to walk a bit?" He wasn't ready for the evening to end, and he liked the warmth of her arm pressed against his.

"Sure."

They meandered down the block and ended up at the park in the heart of downtown. Kayla pulled him toward the fountain. "This fountain is famous in Oak Knoll."

"Why's that?"

"All the money that people toss into the water goes to help local families in need." She pulled a coin from her purse, turned around and tossed it over her shoulder, then handed him a quarter. "Your turn."

He copied her. The coin landed with a plop.

She laughed and her eyes twinkled in the light of the streetlamps.

He pushed a strand of hair away from her face and feathered his thumb across her cheek. "Everything about tonight has been incredible." He lowered his lips to hers and hesitated only a moment before claiming her lips in a gentle kiss.

Chapter 5

Kayla awoke to sunlight streaming into her bedroom. Her thoughts immediately went to Derek and a smile tugged at her lips.

"Good morning, sleepyhead."

Kayla twisted to face her bedroom door. "Mom, you're home. When did you get in?"

"An hour ago. I'm gone a month and suddenly you turn into a sloth. Don't you need to get to the shop?"

Kayla pushed up and settled her pillow behind her back. "What time is it?"

"Nine."

Kayla's heart rate accelerated as she tossed the covers to the side. "Will you call Jill and let her know I'm running late?"

"Sure thing, sweetie. We can talk when you get home. Based on that dreamy smile I spotted, I'd say you have a story to share."

Kayla paused at her closet. "How was your trip? I didn't

know you were coming home or I would have met your plane." She grabbed a skirt and blouse from her closet, then rushed into the bathroom and closed the door. She flipped on the shower and willed it to warm fast while she pulled her hair into a ponytail.

"No worries. I took the red-eye and didn't want to bother you. My trip was perfect." Mom's voice filtered through the door. "I may go back to Florida sooner rather than later. I met someone."

Kayla's hands froze in midair. "Really? Maybe you should stop by at lunch today. We could grab a bite, and you can tell me all about him." She set the brush on the counter.

"I'd like that. And you can tell me about that smile."

Kayla ignored her mom's suggestion and hopped into the shower. She hurried through her morning routine and sat down to apply a light coat of makeup. She hadn't gone to bed until one, and it had taken forever for her to fall asleep. Her mind would not shut down after Derek's kiss. And, oh, what a kiss that was. Perfect in every sense of the word. It was as though he'd read her mind.

A glance at the clock told her she would make it before the store opened, but just barely. Too bad she'd forgotten to set the alarm. Now she'd have to wait until lunch to hear about the man in her mom's life. She hadn't so much as looked at another man since Dad died four years ago, and the curiosity was almost too much to handle.

Undoubtedly Mom had turned more than a few heads with her model good looks and sweet spirit. Trim body, chin-length dark hair, high cheekbones, long legs and large eyes—and Mom always dressed to impress. It was a wonder a man hadn't snatched her up sooner.

Kayla flung the door open and rushed into the kitchen, where her mom sat at the counter holding a mug. "Oh, good, you made coffee." She pulled a travel mug from the cupboard and filled it.

"Yes, and there's a muffin in the bag. I bought an extra one at the airport."

"Thanks." Kayla grabbed the bag and placed a kiss on her mom's cheek as she passed by. "See you at noon."

Ten minutes later she rushed into the flower shop, which Jill had opened early—odd.

"Oh, good, you're here. When your mom called and said you'd be late, I panicked."

"Sorry. I had a late night and overslept."

Jill gasped. "That's right! I want details. How was your date?"

"Great. We had a steak dinner and talked for hours."

"And?" Jill waggled her brow.

"And he's kind of a secretive guy. We talked and talked, but he is still somewhat of a mystery."

"How so?" Jill leaned over and rested her elbows on the counter and propped her chin on her fisted hands.

"From about high school to present there's a black hole he won't talk about. I tried, but he's tight-lipped."

"Hmm. Maybe he was in prison."

"Really? That's what you come up with." Kayla shook her head and set about her normal opening routine. "Is everything ready for the bow wedding tonight?"

"All except for the setup. The wedding is at seven, so I asked Charlie to be here by four-thirty."

A woman walked in and meandered around the gift side of the store. Before long there were several customers browsing and someone who wanted to buy flowers. Saturdays tended to be busy, and today was not an exception. She only hoped she'd be able to run next door for a quick lunch with her mom. She couldn't wait to hear about her man. The morning passed quickly, and right at noon her mom glided in wearing a long, flowing skirt and a sleeveless top that showed off her new tan.

"Mom, aren't you freezing?"

"Only a little. I left my coat in the car and didn't want to go back for it. Are you ready?"

"Yes, hold on a second while I tell Jill." She strode into the workroom. "I'm going next door for lunch with my mom. If you need me, I have my cell."

"Sure thing." Jill dried her hands and followed her into the store. "Welcome home, Olivia."

"Thanks, Jill. How's the flower business?"

"Brisk. Enjoy your lunch."

"We will." Kayla wrapped her arm through her mom's and pulled her from the store. "I'm so hungry."

"Didn't you like the muffin?"

"I didn't have time to eat. It's a good thing I had a huge dinner last night, or I'd be famished."

They pushed into the deli and placed their orders, then found a seat at one of the small tables scattered around the dining area.

"So tell me about this man." Kayla popped a chip into her mouth and listened as her mom shared about her vacation and how she met Stan. He was an attorney in his fifties, widowed, with three grown children and his own practice in Orlando.

"We met at Epcot. He was dining at the same French restaurant as me and struck up a conversation. And as they say, the rest is history."

"He sounds like a catch, Mom. But what about Dad?"

Mom's eyes widened. "What about him?"

"I suppose it's not really about him. After he died and you never started dating, I thought either he was your one and only or you didn't want to go there again since things were rocky."

"Whatever gave you that idea? I know we didn't express our love in front of you, but I loved your father. Our marriage wasn't perfect, but a perfect marriage doesn't exist."

"Then why haven't you gotten back out there?"

Mom shrugged. "I was content to be alone."

Kayla swallowed the lump in her throat. "What changed?"

"I met someone who makes me not want to be alone anymore." Her eyes glowed.

Had Mom fallen in love?

Their sandwiches were delivered with a side cup of cream of broccoli soup. Kayla offered a blessing for the food and focused on eating her soup.

Mom picked up her turkey sandwich. "You still haven't told me about that smile I saw this morning."

Kayla's hand stilled. She met her mom's eyes. "I met someone, too."

Mom flashed a smile and leaned forward. "Tell me about him. Does he mark off all the requirements on your list?"

"I don't know yet." *But he sure is a good kisser.* He'd surprised her last night with his toe-curling kiss. She closed her eyes and still felt his soft lips brushing hers. His touch so gentle, yet strong. He'd drawn her closer and deepened the kiss, then held her, resting his head on hers. The perfect ending to a lovely night. She sighed.

Mom chuckled. "You've got it bad. I'd like to meet this man."

"And I need to meet Stan."

Footsteps approached.

"Jill said I'd find you here."

Kayla whirled around, her heart skipping into overdrive. *Derek.* His azure eyes sparkled in spite of the dreary day and artificial lights of the deli.

* * *

Derek stood beside their table holding a sack. He offered a hand to Kayla's mother. "I'm Derek Wood."

Her mom took his hand. "Olivia Russell."

"Kayla said you'd be back any day."

"Mom surprised me. I had no idea she'd be standing in my doorway when I woke this morning."

"Grab a chair and join us." Olivia motioned toward another table with an empty seat.

"I don't want to intrude."

She smiled sweetly. "But you were looking for my daughter, so you must need to speak with her. I have a better idea. Please take my seat. I have errands to run, anyway." She pushed back and stood. "It was nice meeting you, Derek. I hope the next time our paths cross, I won't be in a rush." She strolled away, and right before she left the room, she turned and wiggled her fingers.

Kayla blinked and shook her head. "What happened to my quiet, unassuming mother? That was *not* the woman who left for Florida a month ago."

He chuckled. "I wondered. She wasn't how I'd pictured her after you talked about her last night. But the two of you could be sisters."

"I know. Mom carries her age well. But I've always thought she was way prettier than me. She has a timeless beauty about her."

"Just like her daughter." He winked.

She raised her palm. "Please don't flatter me. What did you need?"

"I came into town for takeout and wanted to stop in and say hi."

Kayla grinned. "That's nice of you. How's Helen doing today?"

"She's a little tired. I think she may have tried to wait

up for me. I found her asleep on the couch when I got home last night. Otherwise, she's doing well."

"I'm glad. Sorry she waited up, though." She yawned.

He chuckled. "Tired?"

"Nope, all this talk about sleeping makes me yawn."

"Did you have a nice visit with your mom? I really didn't mean to chase her away."

"Yes, we had a very nice talk. And don't worry. She wouldn't have left if she didn't want to."

He sensed there was more but didn't want to intrude. Sure, they'd shared a perfect evening together last night, but that didn't give him license to invade her private life uninvited. Boundaries were important in any relationship. Did they have a *relationship*? Maybe not yet, but at this rate they were well on their way. He wasn't sure that was what he needed in his life right now, but he wouldn't close off the possibility, either.

"You okay?" Kayla placed her hand on his.

He nodded. "I should be going." He slid his hand out from under hers and stood.

Kayla hopped up. "I'll walk you out. I need to get back to work, anyway."

Derek pulled the door open. "After you."

"Thanks." She breezed past, then waited, a soft smile touching her lips. "I just thought of something. I'm on the Spring Festival committee. May I recruit you to help?"

He liked giving back, but was now the right time with his mom's health scare? "I don't know."

She raised a hand. "Before you say no, I understand you're busy taking care of your mom, but I promise this won't take a lot of your time."

"That might work, then. Maybe we can get together later and discuss what you have in mind."

"Sure. We close at four tonight. Jill booked a wedding,

so we're closing early. Lucky me—I don't need to be there. I can meet you at Java World, my treat. They make the best mochas in town."

"How could I say no to that offer?" He grinned and headed to his pickup.

His cell buzzed in his pocket. "Hey, Jerry. What's up?" His manager had given him the space he'd asked for, but if his frequent calls the past couple of weeks were any indication, that was over.

"When are you coming back?"

"I'm not. I told you that." Derek jumped into his truck and closed the door so no eavesdroppers would hear their conversation.

"I know what you said, but I need you in LA."

"Not now. I need to be with my mom."

"This is a mistake, Derek. People will forget about you if you're not in the public eye or putting out albums."

"Let them forget." He rested his head against the side window.

"You don't mean that, so I won't hold it against you. I have a strong feeling you'll be back here sooner than you realize. You just need the right motivation."

"Not gonna happen. And what do you mean, right motivation?"

Silence.

"Jerry?" Since when did his manager hang up on him? A sick feeling gripped his stomach. What was Jerry up to?

Chapter 6

Kayla locked up the flower shop, then darted across the street at exactly four o'clock. The day had dragged ever since she'd seen Derek at lunch. All she could think about was seeing him again.

She pulled open the glass door that led into Java World. The rich aroma of coffee scented the air and put a smile on her face. She looked to her left toward the dimly lit dining area where assorted tables and chairs were laid out—no Derek. Her gaze landed on the walls, where artwork created by local artists hung, each highlighted with its own mini light. It was always fun to see the revolving gallery of sorts.

She stepped into the short line directly in front of her, focusing on the chalkboard listing today's special as a white mocha.

"Hey," a male voice said softly into her ear.

She startled and whirled around holding a hand over her heart. "Derek! I didn't hear you come in."

He grinned. "What are you having?"

She pointed to the special on the board. "How about you?"

"Sounds great. Think I'll have the same."

She ordered their coffees. "We pick them up at the other end," Kayla said over her shoulder. A few minutes later they each held a steaming mug of chocolaty goodness. She led the way to a table near the back where they were less likely to be interrupted.

They slid into their seats and Derek took a sip from the large navy mug with Java World's logo. "Mmm. You were right. They do make good mochas."

"How is your mom doing?"

"Not bad. She's back to work. Her business is home based, so that's made it very convenient for her. She probably wouldn't have been able to go back to work so soon if she worked in an office."

"That's great. I'm happy her recovery is going so well. How's her speech?"

"Not normal yet and better in the mornings than evenings, when she's tired."

"That makes sense."

She rested her chin on the palm of her hand. "As you know, the Spring Festival is the biggest event we hold in Oak Knoll, so we go all out. I'm in charge of entertainment. We always have face painting and various booths for the kids to play games. Last year we rented inflatables, which were a big hit. My budget is larger this year, so I'm considering bringing in miniature ponies, as well. What do you think?"

"Any kid would be thrilled. What do you do for the teens?"

She bit her bottom lip. The teenagers always slipped through the cracks, and she had no idea what to do. "In the past, several of them have manned the kiddie stations. What do you suggest? My budget is gone unless I don't do the ponies."

"I suggest skipping the ponies. What about a dunk tank or movie in the park?"

She pulled a notepad and pen from her purse and wrote his suggestion down. "It's too cold for a dunk tank, but the movie could work. It'd have to be family friendly, though. What other ideas do you have?"

"What about a concert with a local band?"

She shook her head. "We've done that in the past. There should be someone working on that already."

"You may have the teens covered, then, if the band is good."

"Margie, the festival coordinator, usually gets the same group every year and they're not bad."

He chuckled. "*Not bad* isn't exactly a glowing review."

She shrugged. "I imagine *not bad* is all this town can afford."

"Where do I fit into this?" He sipped his mocha.

"I'm not sure exactly." Her face heated. She'd indicated that she had a job for him only because she'd wanted an excuse to spend time with him. "There's a committee to make sure all of this happens."

"What do you do during the festival?"

"Hopefully nothing. I try to plan to the nth degree, but if someone doesn't show for a shift, I find a substitute. Honestly, I'm pretty busy at the flower shop during the festival. All the stores run a special sale, and I'm stuck at the register much of the time."

"How about you put me down as a substitute? If you need someone to fill in, let me know."

"Really? That's nice of you. I was thinking more behind the scenes. Like maybe setup, but I like your idea."

The only problem was she wouldn't get to spend any extra time with him if that was all he did. Her cell rang. "I'm sorry." She pulled it from her purse and frowned. "I need to take this. It's the festival coordinator."

"No problem."

"Hi, Margie. What's up?"

"The mayor wants to do a parade this year! Can you believe it?"

"A parade?" Kayla wasn't sure if that was a good thing or a bad thing. It would definitely complicate things.

"Yes, and he wants all the businesses to enter floats."

Kayla groaned. "How am I supposed to coordinate the entertainment, run a business *and* create a parade float? It's impossible."

"I know it will be a challenge for the smaller businesses, but I'm sure you could get volunteers to help."

Kayla's stomach knotted. This was *not* what she'd signed up for.

"There's one more thing," Margie said. "I don't know how we could hold a parade with the bounce house and obstacle course inflatables set up on Main Street. It would be a logistical nightmare."

"What are you saying exactly?"

"Nix the inflatables."

"But they were a huge hit last year. We saw more foot traffic than ever before, which translates into sales for the downtown district." She clenched and unclenched her hand. A technique she'd learned as a teen to help release tension.

Derek reached across the table and rested his hand over her fist. "I have an idea," he said quietly.

"Margie, may I call you back?"

"Sure, but the parade is a go. I'll be sending out emails to all the downtown businesses."

"Okay." She disconnected the call and returned her attention to Derek. "What's your idea?"

"You could put the playthings for the kids in the park. There's plenty of green space. The parade will draw more foot traffic than you've ever seen at one time." He gave her hand a squeeze before releasing it. "And I'll help with your float."

The park was actually a decent idea. A smile stretched her lips. "Great idea—thanks! I could kiss you right now!" Her cheeks burned as her comment registered in her mind.

"I won't stop you." He waggled his brow.

Her thoughts immediately shot to their kiss last night. She buried her face in her hands.

Derek chuckled as he pried her fingers away from her face. "I was teasing. But in all seriousness, you can kiss me anytime." He shot a cheeky grin her way.

Kayla made a face and rose. "You ready to get out of here?"

"Yep." He got up and held out his hand.

She slipped her fingers through his.

He spoke softly into her ear as they left Java World. "I meant it when I said I'd like to help with the float. Keep me in the loop. Okay?" He stopped walking and they stood facing each other on the sidewalk.

"I will, and thanks." She looked into his eyes and her heart tripped as she realized she could see them in a serious relationship if things continued to progress as they were. Then again, maybe this was infatuation. She definitely liked him, but she didn't know him all that well. He was such a mystery.

He pressed a kiss to her forehead. "If you're not too busy, we could do something Friday night. Maybe dinner and movie?"

"I'd like that." Her skin tingled from his touch.

"I'll call you."

"DJ!"

"Oh no," Derek groaned. He gently grasped Kayla's shoulders and looked directly into her eyes.

Kayla's heart beat wildly and fear gripped her. The look in Derek's eyes scared her, more than the idea of building a float.

"Whatever happens next, know that everything I've told you is the truth. I really like you, Kayla." He released her shoulders and turned toward a woman who kept calling out to someone named DJ.

Kayla moved to get a better view of a petite woman with long blond hair and gasped. "Oh my goodness!" She looked exactly like Estelle Rogers. Kayla was a fan of her movies, except that last one she'd done was awful. What was *she* doing in Oregon?

Derek's heart beat double time as Estelle stormed toward him, her ridiculously high heels clicking on the sidewalk.

Kayla grabbed his arm. "That's Estelle Rogers! I love her movies! How do you know her?"

"It's kind of a long story."

Estelle stopped a couple of feet from him and glared. "It's about time I found you. Your mother said you were in town. Why didn't you answer my calls?"

"Kayla Russell, meet Estelle Rogers."

Kayla held out her hand. "It's an honor to meet you. I'm a big fan."

"Thanks. Be a dear and run along. I need to have a word with my boyfriend."

Derek cringed. "Ex-boyfriend, Estelle." Kayla shifted beside him and he turned to face her. He grasped her hand and gave it a gentle squeeze.

The light that had shone in Kayla's eyes was gone, and in its place confusion resided. "You have a girlfriend? Why is she calling you DJ?"

"Estelle isn't my girlfriend. We broke up more than six months ago." His stomach tightened. What a mess! "I'll call you and explain everything later. Okay, Kayla?"

Estelle laughed and looped her arm through his. "DJ, stop toying with this girl. You know you're mine. It's time you came home. Your fans miss you." She batted her lashes and smiled her I'm-a-star-and-everyone-loves-me smile.

"Fans?" Kayla's face paled. She looked from Estelle to him. Her eyes widened. "Oh my goodness! I can't believe I was so blind. I understand what's going on. Don't bother calling, *DJ*." She said his name as if it were a dirty word, then turned and jogged across the street and disappeared inside her florist shop.

His stomach sickened as he rounded on Estelle. "What are you doing here and how did you find me?" He kept his voice low. "I blocked your number for a reason. We are over. Done. Kaput."

Estelle waved a hand and shook her head. "Jerry told me where you were. Don't be a child. We had a spat. That's no reason for you to disappear and block me from your life."

He rubbed his neck. "I can't believe this."

"Believe it, baby, because I'm here to bring you back with me. LA isn't the same without you. I need you in my life."

Now he understood Jerry's prediction that he'd be back in Los Angeles soon. He worked to control his anger and kept his voice cool. "Right. Like you needed all those other men. I'm only a distraction in your downtime. Someone to stroke your enormous ego."

"Give me a break." She looked over her shoulder. "Behave yourself. The paparazzi will be here any minute."

"Where is your bodyguard?"

"I didn't think I'd need him here, so I gave him a couple of days off."

Derek narrowed his eyes as he spotted two well-known and aggressive photographers running toward them. "Not a smart move. You brought them here. *You* deal with them." He spun around and jogged to his pickup, but before he could pull out, Estelle hopped into the passenger seat holding her spiky shoes.

"This is perfect. They're going to eat this up." She feigned a look of surprise and raised her hands to supposedly block their shot.

He rolled his eyes and tore away from the curb. "Where's your car? I'll drop you off."

"And leave me alone with *them*? No way! Please, let's find a quiet place to talk. You have no idea what your disappearance did to my career."

"Nor do I care." He spotted her Mercedes on a side street and slowed.

"Please, DJ, I'm begging you." She rested a hand on his arm, her voice panicked. "I know I shouldn't have ambushed you like I did, and yes, I made an anonymous call about you and me being here, but please don't leave me alone with them. You know how they freak me out."

His heart softened. Estelle's love-hate relationship with the paparazzi was no secret to him or anyone who knew her. She needed to stay in the public eye for her career, but their aggressive tactics scared her. "Okay. We'll leave your car here for now. But don't think you're going to wiggle your way back into my life. When I left Los Angeles, I left everything, including you, and I'm not going back."

"I'm not leaving without you. I need you in my life."

A glance in his rearview mirror showed no one following. His shoulders relaxed as they cruised toward his mom's place. "You don't need me. I recall you once calling me eye candy. Seems to me all you want is *eye candy* to parade around with, so don't insult me by pretending you care about me as a person. You never did." He whipped into Mom's long driveway and followed it until he reached the house, which was not visible from the road. He pulled to a stop, took a bracing breath and faced Estelle. Her blond hair curled in soft ringlets around her beautiful face. He'd once loved her. But that was before he realized how shallow she was and that she'd been only using him to further her career. As she was trying to do now. Of all the men she knew, why him?

His face heated. He'd been taken in by her beauty and charm when they'd run into one another after a movie screening two years ago. If he'd only known what kind of person she was then, he'd never have asked her out, even if it did help his career to be seen in public with her.

"I care about you, DJ." She caressed his arm. "We were great together. Give us another chance."

"Stop acting, Estelle. I fell for that once, but I'm not naive anymore. I see right through you." He shook her hand off his arm. She cared about only herself, and it was clear she needed him for her endgame. Or at least, she thought she did; otherwise, she wouldn't be here. "This is how it's going to play out. I'll move back into the guest cottage for the night. You'll stay in my mom's guestroom, and then tomorrow I'll have a friend pick up your car. We'll meet at a preset destination. You will leave, and I will go on with my life."

Her face hardened and she crossed her arms. "I don't think so. I'm not leaving this town until you agree to go with me and announce that you're working on your next album."

He shook his head. “Not happening. I’m done with that life.” He pushed open his door and slid out.

Estelle met him by the hood. “Please, DJ. I need you back.”

“So you said.” He strode toward the front door and looked over his shoulder. “Are you coming?”

“If you won’t return for me, then do it for your fans.” She squared her shoulders and marched forward.

Her words hit their mark. For the most part, he appreciated his fans. They were his only regret.

Estelle glanced at him. “Jerry told me about your mom. Are you sure it’s okay that I stay here?”

He jerked his head in her direction. “If you knew, why did you come? And why would Jerry tell you where I am? What do you have over him?”

She pursed her lips, and he saw vulnerability in her eyes. “Nothing. He’s my manager, too. Remember? My movie tanked, and he’s trying to help a client. The critics are ripping me apart. Everyone loved us together. Don’t you see? If you and I get back together, then the media will focus on us as a couple and stop obsessing over the movie’s failure. I need some good press. Actually, I need a *lot* of good press so the critics will forget about my last movie and producers will want to hire me again.” She folded her arms. “There, I said it. Happy now?”

He should’ve known it was something like that. “No, but I’m sorry about your movie. How about you lie low for a few days? I’m sure the next big story will pop up any day and talk of your movie will be forgotten.”

“Maybe, but I like my idea better.”

“You always did have to be right.” He pushed the door open and waited for Estelle before closing it. “Mom, I’m home, and I brought a guest.”

“In…the kitchen.”

Estelle grabbed his arm. "Is she okay?"

"She had a stroke and she's tired by evening, so her speech is usually more halting. But don't let that fool you. Her mind is sharp, so don't talk down to her or try to finish her sentences for her. That only frustrates her more."

Estelle nodded and walked beside him into the kitchen. "Mom, this is Estelle Rogers. Estelle, Helen."

Mom turned from the oven. "Welcome. Derek's…told me…all about…you."

"It's lovely to meet you, Helen."

Derek sighed at the excited look in his mom's eyes. Yes, he'd told her about Estelle, but he had left out the unpleasant details. Maybe he should have shared Estelle's true character with her, but it really didn't matter, at least not right now. Estelle would be here only a short time—not nearly enough time to snare his mother in her web of deceit and lies.

Mom held a small casserole dish in one hand. "Dinner is ready." She pointed to the table, which was set for two.

Derek quickly set another place and helped get the food on the table. "Estelle needs a place to stay for a few nights. Do you mind if she sleeps in the guestroom? I will move back into the guesthouse." Since his mom's stroke he felt more comfortable being under the same roof, but as long as Estelle was here…

"She's welcome to stay…as long as…she'd like."

Derek stifled a groan and offered a blessing for the food, then passed the meat loaf to Estelle.

"Thanks." She cut a piece in half and placed it on her plate.

"What brings…you here, Estelle?" Mom asked.

"Your son. I want him to come back to LA with me."

Mom nodded but didn't respond. She'd always excelled at hiding her thoughts when she wanted to.

What was he going to do? He knew his ex-girlfriend well enough to know she meant it when she said she wouldn't leave without him, but there was no way that would happen. His life was here—at least for now. His mother needed him. Plus he'd said he'd help Kayla with her float, and he intended to keep his word. That is, if she'd let him. After the look of disappointment he'd seen on her face as she ran away, he had doubts.

Chapter 7

Kayla sat on the couch and stared at the television. A photo of Estelle Rogers and Derek played on the screen. The hosts declared the duo had been spotted together and speculated they were an item once again.

She pushed the power button.

Her mom walked into the room holding a plate. "I made dinner. Better grab some while it's hot."

"Thanks, but I'm not hungry."

"I don't suppose your loss of appetite has anything to do with what happened outside Java World this evening?"

Her gaze shot to her mother's. "You know about Derek?"

Mom nodded. "I think the whole town is talking about it. Those photographers were asking all sorts of questions about Derek after he drove off with the movie star. One even went so far as to offer money to anyone who would give him the address of where Derek is staying. But no one would tell him." She smiled smugly. "Helen doesn't need all that craziness at her house. Poor woman has had enough trouble of late. I still can't believe she had a stroke."

Her mom's words rang true. Helen absolutely couldn't deal with all the attention that her son's fame could bring to her doorstep. She studied her mother's serene face. She wanted that kind of contentment, but turmoil and anger ran rampant through Kayla. "How could I have been so naive?"

"What do you mean?"

"I knew Derek looked like DJ Parker, yet I talked myself out of believing there was a connection. I never imagined a famous singer would live here. I feel so stupid." She rested her chin on her tucked knees. "Estelle and Derek are probably having a good laugh at my expense right now." Her stomach knotted even tighter.

"I love you with all my heart, Kayla, but the world does not revolve around you. Derek seemed like a very nice man to me, and I think it's safe to say he is not laughing at your expense. Have you asked him about it?"

Her mom's words stung. "No, and I don't plan to, either." Mom was supposed to be on her side. Why was she defending Derek?

"You may want to reconsider. I know his fame took you by surprise, honey, but I've never seen you take to a man like you did him. I think the two of you have a connection. If I were you, I wouldn't toss that away so easily."

"He should've told me he was DJ Parker."

"Maybe." Mom placed her glass on the side table. "It must be difficult being famous. I imagine it's tough to know who your real friends are." She bit into a dinner roll.

Mom made a good point, but that didn't excuse the fact that Derek had kept his singing career quiet. She knew there were things he wasn't sharing about himself, but he should have told her he was DJ Parker when they were listening to his album. Instead he'd stayed silent. In a way she understood his silence, but didn't he see that since she liked him before she knew he was famous, it would have been safe to reveal his secret to her?

Kayla stretched out her legs. "He said he'd help with the float for the flower shop. I doubt that will happen now, but I don't see how we can pull it off without him."

"This is news. What are you talking about?"

Kayla explained about the parade and the mayor's request, then sighed. "I have too much to do. I really don't see how I will get everything done."

"Your family and friends will pitch in and together we all will make it happen."

Tears pricked Kayla's eyes. "Thanks, Mom. You have no idea what a relief that is. I'm sure Jill's family will pitch in, too." A weight lifted and she grinned. "You have always been the voice of reason in my life. Thank you."

Mom held a hand across her heart and ducked her chin. "I'm always here for you. Now go make yourself a plate of food."

Kayla stood. "Yes, ma'am. What about your attorney friend? Will he be coming for the Spring Festival?"

"Stan is a very busy man, but I'll invite him. I'd like the two of you to meet."

"Good." As Kayla strolled into the kitchen, her cell phone rang. She touched the accept button. "Hello?"

"I'm so glad you picked up. I was afraid after what happened earlier you wouldn't."

The sound of Derek's baritone voice made her stomach flip-flop. "What can I do for you?" Regardless of everything, she couldn't bring herself to be rude to him.

"I was hoping we could talk."

"We're talking now."

"Right. What I meant was I'd like to take you out to dinner and explain everything."

"No explanation is necessary."

"I disagree."

Kayla huffed out a breath. "I suppose you're used to people giving in to your whims, but I'm not one of those people." That sounded harsher than she'd intended, but she wouldn't take the words back, because they were true. She ripped a dinner roll from the bag and tossed it onto a plate, then flicked a spoonful of mashed potatoes beside it.

"Okay. I get it." His tone was dejected. "You're angry and that's justified, but I like you, Kayla, and I still want to help with the festival if you'll allow me."

Kayla stilled. "Okay."

"Okay?"

"Yes."

"Great. I'll draw up a few designs and bring them by your shop."

"Not that I don't appreciate the help, but are you sure you have the time for this? I mean, with Estelle here and all." She held her breath.

"I want to do this. Besides, she won't be taking up my time."

She let out her breath in a soft whoosh. "Okay. Thanks. But don't go crazy. Whatever we do needs to be cheap and easy."

"Got it. See you soon."

It seemed Derek wasn't out of her life as she'd presumed. But whatever romantic notions she'd had for him needed to be squelched. She refused to put her heart in the hands of a man who would eventually leave and take it with him.

Derek strode into the flower shop and spotted Kayla with a customer. No matter. That would give him time to duck into the back before the paparazzi spotted him through the window. He'd thought for sure after a week they'd have given up, but apparently Estelle was getting what she wanted—publicity that didn't involve her movie. He pushed through the swinging doors and stopped.

Jill stood by the back door in the arms of a dark-haired man the size of an NFL linebacker. He cleared his throat and she whipped her head toward him.

"What are you doing in here?"

"Hiding. What are *you* doing?"

She stepped out of the man's arms. "This is Charlie. He delivers the flowers. Charlie, Derek is our resident celebrity."

Charlie held out a beefy hand. "The whole town's been talking about you."

Derek suppressed a groan. "Maybe going back to LA isn't such a bad idea after all."

"Don't you dare leave." Jill scowled. "My business partner would be impossible if you disappeared from her life."

He stood a little taller. Kayla would miss him? And here he'd thought he'd ruined everything.

Jill glanced toward the closed door leading to the front of the store. "About what you saw when you walked in—do you think you could keep that between the three of us? Kayla doesn't know about Charlie and me yet, and I don't think now is a good time to tell her."

"I don't know. She's already unhappy with me."

Jill frowned. "Good point. I like you, Derek, and you're good for my friend. Don't lie—just don't offer the information. Deal?"

"I suppose. But you won't be able to keep this from her for long. What if she'd been the one who walked in and saw the two of you?"

Charlie wrapped his hand around Jill's. "He's right. There's really no point in keeping us a secret any longer now that—"

"Okay." Jill whirled around, disengaged her hand from his and pushed him toward the back door. "Those flowers need to be delivered. You better get a move on."

"Okey-dokey." He nodded to Derek, then slipped out the back door.

Derek wondered what the man had been about to say, but Kayla pushed through the door. She looked ravishing. Her hair was piled atop her head with a few wisps dangling beside her smooth cheeks. Her lips stretched into a polite smile.

"I see you've made yourself at home."

"Sorry about that. I didn't want the paparazzi to see me and cause a ruckus, so I thought I'd dart back here."

Jill sidled up to him. "It's no big deal, Kayla. How about I take over in front for a bit, while the two of you talk float designs?" She rushed toward the door and looked over her shoulder.

He mouthed a thank-you.

Jill grinned and left.

He pulled out three sheets of folded paper he'd stuffed into his back jeans pocket and handed them to Kayla. "They're rough, but I think you'll get the idea." He rocked back on his heels as she unfolded and studied the designs he'd spent hours on.

"They're amazing, but they're not simple." She shook her head. "I don't think we could pull any of these off. Even if we had the man-hours, we don't have the money."

"Then let the float be my treat."

"No way."

"Why? You have something against a philanthropic former singer?"

"Of course not. Wait—former singer? What are you talking about?"

"I left the business."

"Does *the business* know that? Because from what I've seen on TV, you're as hot as ever."

She watched gossip shows? He'd pictured her listening to music and reading books in her off time, not planted in front of the television screen. "I'd like to explain all of that, if you'd give me a chance."

"It doesn't matter. And since there aren't any other philanthropists tossing money my way, I don't see that we have much choice but to accept your offer."

"Don't sound so excited." He tried to curb the sarcasm in his tone but failed miserably.

"Hey, I didn't ask for your help with the float."

"Maybe not, but you sure didn't turn me down, either."

"Okay, fine, but I didn't know who you were then. I thought you were an ordinary guy. Not a famous singer."

"You have something against famous people?"

"No. Only you!" She crossed her arms and spun away from him.

He felt sucker punched. Her words hit their mark, but he refused to let her win. He cared about Kayla and the people in this town. He would not allow her to cut him out just because he had a life before he came here.

He stepped across the room until he was close enough to rest a hand on her shoulder. "Why me?"

"Because you humiliated me," she said softly, and turned to face him.

The hurt in her eyes made his gut tighten. "I'm so sorry. I didn't mean to hurt you." He didn't understand what he'd done other than not tell her he was DJ Parker. Could that be why she was so upset? Whatever it was, it didn't matter right now. He just wanted back in Kayla's life—wanted their friendship back, wanted to continue getting to know her. "Please forgive me and let me help you." He longed to caress her soft cheeks and kiss her until she forgot about the pain he'd caused her, but he forced his hands to his sides.

She looked into his eyes and something changed. The hurt was gone, but something new was in its place. "Okay. I would appreciate your help."

"Yes." He pumped a fist. "You won't regret this." He spread the designs out on the worktable and explained his vision for each one.

They tossed around the pros and cons of the designs and ended up deciding on his simplest idea. He'd pull a flatbed trailer decked out in a flower garden with a stone bench under an arch.

Kayla made a copy of the design and handed him the original. "I'll take care of the flowers if you can deal with the rest. I'll get you the names and numbers of everyone I think would be willing to help."

"Thanks. About dinner?"

She wrinkled her nose. "I don't think that'd be a good idea with your girlfriend in town."

"I told you Estelle is *not* my girlfriend."

"That's not what *she* says."

He raked a hand through his hair. "Who are you going to believe? A woman you don't know or a man you do know?"

Kayla raised a brow as if to question whether she knew him. She walked toward the door that divided the work-room from the storefront. "No worries, Derek. You don't owe me an explanation. We had a nice time together, and now I'd like to keep things between us professional."

He rushed forward. "But I really like you, Kayla. I want to see where this leads between us."

She shook her head. "I don't think so. We'll work together on this project, but that's it."

There was no use arguing now. But if it was the last thing he did, he'd find a way to get her to change her mind about him.

Chapter 8

The Flowers and More delivery van drove up Derek's driveway and stopped about fifty feet from where he worked on the float. He slid the hammer into his tool belt and waved.

Charlie got out and sauntered in his direction. "The women asked me to stop in and see how things are going."

The screen door slammed. Derek looked over his shoulder and winced. Estelle stood there with crossed arms.

Charlie's startled eyes slammed into his. "Why is she still here?" He kept his voice low. "I heard she'd left town a week ago."

"She was lying low for a few days, and it's turned into a week. Honestly, I don't know how to get rid of her. But she's great company for my mom, especially since she's only working part-time."

"I get that about your mom and all, but I thought you had a thing for Kayla. You better not be messing with her."

He planted his feet in a wide stance and folded his arms across his chest.

Derek raised his hands palms out. "There is nothing going on between Estelle and me. Not that it matters. Kayla's done a one eighty on me and is keeping her distance. Were it not for the float…"

"I wouldn't be so sure about that. She downloaded most of your songs to her MP3 player. She walks around the shop humming them all the time."

Derek grinned. "I didn't know that." Maybe he had a chance with her after all.

"A-hem."

He glanced back toward the house again. "What do you need, Estelle?"

"Your mother asked me to send you for groceries." She waved a piece of paper. "Here's her list."

Charlie chuckled. "I don't envy you, man."

Derek shook his head, walked up the steps of the porch and took the list from Estelle. "When I finish up here, I'll head into town."

Estelle stuck her nose in the air, spun around, then went back inside without even acknowledging Charlie.

Derek headed back to the driveway. "Sorry about that. She's still angry that I refuse to return to LA with her and takes every chance she gets to let me know her feelings." Like what she thought mattered to him. She was the last person he would return to his old life for. She'd burned him, and he wasn't going down that road again.

Derek walked over to the trailer he'd begun to build the float on. "What do you think so far?"

"I think you better work faster. The parade is in five weeks."

"Don't worry—it will be finished in plenty of time."

He undid his tool belt and brushed his hands on his jeans. "Guess I'd better go shopping or risk starving tonight."

Charlie clapped him on the shoulder as if he were one of the guys in the football locker room. "What should I tell Jill and Kayla?"

He rubbed the spot Charlie had slapped. "Whatever you say, don't tell them about Estelle."

"I meant about the float."

"Right. Tell them it's coming along."

"Will do. Want help later? I should be off early and could be here by four."

"Sure."

Charlie waved and slid behind the wheel of the delivery van. He tooted the horn before backing up and heading to the main road.

Derek rounded the house and stopped short when he spotted Estelle sitting in the shade of an old oak tree. Her legs were crossed at the ankles and his mom's snow-white cat rested in her lap. He hadn't seen the cat around much lately and wondered where it'd been.

Estelle's voice traveled through the quiet yard. "What a sweet kitty you are." She sighed as if the weight of the world rested on her shoulders and stroked the cat's back. "My life is such a mess. I don't know what I'm going to do. You are so lucky you're a cat and not a person. All you need to worry about is your next meal."

He frowned. What was Estelle talking about? He kicked at a pebble to alert her of his presence and fully rounded the corner.

She brushed the cat from her lap and jumped to standing. "I thought you went shopping." Her brow puckered and a hint of pink tinged her cheeks.

"I need my wallet." He brushed by her and didn't look

back. Unease at what he'd overheard propelled him to the guest cottage. What was *really* going on with Estelle?

Later that afternoon, Derek spotted Charlie pulling into the driveway, but this time another vehicle followed. Kayla stepped out of a black hatchback. A cool look covered her face.

"How's it going?" Charlie asked.

Derek shot him a questioning look, then grinned at Kayla. "Great. How are you, Kayla?"

"Fine." She brushed past him and hustled toward the float.

So this was how it was going to be? Disappointment washed through him. He missed their camaraderie and her playfulness. He'd hoped they'd gotten past the wall she'd erected since Estelle's arrival, but he'd been mistaken. He squared his shoulders.

Charlie sidled up to him and said in a low voice, "I'm really sorry, man, but I let it slip that Estelle is staying here. I feel awful. It was a complete accident."

"Don't worry about it. You probably did me a favor in the long run. Now I don't need to worry about Kayla finding out." The less-than-friendly attitude from Kayla made sense now. No matter—he'd win her over one way or another. Surely she'd understand Estelle's situation. He bumped shoulders with Kayla. "What do you think?"

"It looks like a trailer with a couple of wood frames on top of it," she said drily.

"That's pretty much what I have so far. I still need to finish the arbor. But the bridge is complete. I still need to get a bench for whoever ends up riding on the float."

Her head whipped toward him. "Wait. Who's going to ride on the float? We didn't discuss that."

He shrugged. "It's an option, should someone *want* to ride. Nothing to worry about."

"Oh, okay. Will it be ready in time?"

He laid a hand across his heart. "You doubt me?"

"Sorry, but I need to make sure." A hint of a smile played at her lips.

"You can trust me, Kayla."

Her expression turned stony. "Mmm-hmm."

The screen door to the house banged shut. "Your mom wants you to invite your guests inside." Estelle delivered the proclamation with a smug smile.

What was the woman up to now? Much to his chagrin, she'd actually taken to his mom and the two were good company for each other. Not that their getting along made things any easier for him.

Kayla faced him, brows raised. "Charlie said she was still here. What's up with that?"

"She's unhappy and stubborn. I suppose there's a small part of me that feels sorry for her, too. She's going through a rough patch. Besides, my mom likes her company."

Kayla's eyes held indifference. "Are you going to invite us in, like she requested?"

"In a minute." He lowered his voice. "Why do things between us have to change, Kayla?"

Her eyes widened. "Aside from the fact you weren't up-front with me, which I kind of understand, there's no point. Eventually you're going to get bored with this small town and move back to LA and your exciting singing career." She marched past him without giving him a chance to respond.

The last place Kayla wanted to be was in close proximity to both Estelle and Derek, but she refused to let him see how the woman's presence rattled her, and the best way to do that was act as though she weren't bothered.

"Are you sure you want to go in there?" Derek asked.

Kayla raised her chin. "Yes."

"Okay, then. After you, milady." He grasped her hand as she tried to slide past him.

She raised their entwined hands. "Are you sure this is a good idea?"

"I'm not sure about a lot of things, but one thing I do know is that I want to hold your hand."

Kayla held back a smile. "Come on, Charlie," she tossed over her shoulder. She stepped into the tidy home and immediately spotted Helen in an easy chair and Estelle sitting on the worn leather couch nearest Helen in the front room. Large windows looked out to the area where they'd stood seconds ago.

Estelle beamed a smile at Derek. He grimaced, released Kayla's hand and motioned for her to sit in the center of the couch as he sat on the opposite end from Estelle. If Kayla hadn't been so annoyed, she'd have felt sorry for him. The only other seat in the room was across from Helen. She couldn't take that and force Charlie's large frame to cram between Estelle and Derek. With aplomb she parked herself on the couch between the two.

"Excuse me, Kayla—" Estelle flashed a winning smile "—but would you mind switching spots with me?"

A rough laugh escaped Kayla's lips, and she started to move, but Derek snagged her hand.

"Kayla isn't moving."

Derek's firm declaration sent prickles of delight shooting through Kayla.

Estelle frowned and an awkward silence settled in the room.

Charlie leaned forward and rested his elbows on

his knees. "How is your recovery coming along, Mrs. Wood?"

The conversation continued and the tension in the room dwindled some. Kayla breathed a little easier now that conversation flowed.

Twenty minutes later the three of them headed out to the yard. Derek's mom was a sweetheart, but she seemed taken in by Estelle. Surely she could see through the woman. Why Derek allowed her to stay here escaped her understanding. He'd said he felt sorry for her, but what if it was more than that?

What if he still had feelings for Estelle? Kayla couldn't compete with the glamorous movie star. She was just a small-town girl and life here didn't compare to the excitement and adventure the big city held. Eventually Estelle would take him away and his stay would be only a blip on the timeline of his life.

Derek and Charlie walked directly to the float.

"When will we be able to paint it?" Kayla's gaze rested on the unfinished project.

"Next week," Derek said with a grin.

"Good." She spun around. "Call me, and I'll rally the troops. Do you need any more help besides Charlie's to build the arbor?"

"Are you offering your services? I wouldn't turn down your help."

"Not exactly, but if you need me, I'm available. Or I could find you qualified help." She wasn't sure what she wanted him to say. Being here with Estelle nearby made her edgy and reminded her that Derek had another life. One she didn't fit into.

"Thanks, but we have everything covered."

"Oh. Okay." Disappointment washed over her, but she

quickly pasted on a smile. "I'll leave you to it, then. See you guys."

Kayla drove home, her mind a jumble of mixed emotions. Derek acted as if everything were normal between them. Yet she couldn't get past the fact that he was a famous singer. Famous enough he wanted to hide out for a while to find himself, as her mom had put it. But what happened once he did? Would he pack up and move back to Los Angeles?

A few minutes later she pulled into her driveway, set the brake and wandered inside, her mind still mired in confusion and doubt. "Hello! I'm home," she called out.

Silence greeted her. "Mom?" With a shrug, she ambled into the kitchen. Mom must be out with friends. She added fresh water to the teakettle and clicked on the stove. The doorbell pealed. Double-timing it to see who was there, she spotted Jill's car in the driveway. She pulled the door open. "Hey, girl." Since they worked together all day, they rarely spent time socializing.

The deep furrow between Jill's brows made Kayla's stomach twist. "What's wrong?"

"Nothing," She hesitated. "I…need to tell you something." Jill stuffed her hands into the back pockets of her jeans. "Mind if I come inside for a minute?"

She glanced over her shoulder, and for the first time Kayla noticed Charlie sitting in the passenger seat. "Not at all. I just put water on for tea. Let's talk in the kitchen." She led the way and glanced back. "Charlie doesn't mind waiting in the car?"

"No. Actually, he's the reason I'm here."

"Oh?" She pressed her lips together.

"Yes."

The teakettle whistled. Kayla removed it from the

burner, then pulled a teacup and saucer from the cupboard. "Would you like tea?"

"Uh…no, thank you. Will you please sit? All your fidgeting is making me nervous." Jill pulled out a chair and sat.

Kayla left her tea on the counter and did as Jill requested. "You are scaring me. What's wrong?" Her shoulders tightened and she tapped her heel against the floor.

"I'm probably making way too big a deal of this, but I wanted you to know that Charlie and I are dating."

Kayla's foot stilled and her shoulders relaxed. "Oh, that's all? I've suspected there was something going on between you for a while."

"Then you're not angry?"

"Of course not. How could I be? You make a cute couple."

Jill's eyes sparkled. "I think he may be *the one*."

"I hope he is. He's a doll, and you deserve someone who will treat you like a princess. I like Charlie, or I never would have hired him. If you want my blessing, you have it."

"So you're not upset at all? I mean, with what happened with Derek and everything, I thought maybe you might be jealous or feel left out."

Kayla shook her head. "I'm not so self-absorbed that I can't be happy for my friends when they find love. So what if my Prince Charming hasn't dropped into my life yet?" She shrugged.

"You're the best, Kayla!" Jill pulled her into a quick hug. "I'd better go, or Charlie may wonder what's going on. I can let myself out. Say hi to your mom for me." She breezed out and a second later the door clicked closed.

Kayla plopped into a kitchen chair and stared vacantly. She'd meant what she'd said to Jill. She was happy for her and Charlie, but Jill's concern for her love life worried her. Maybe she was destined to be alone forever. Derek's dazzling eyes danced across her mind and she sighed. *He* was not an option—too many unknowns to risk her heart.

Chapter 9

Derek stalked along Mom's driveway to the shed. Estelle's heels clicked a staccato beat as she attempted to keep up. Why wouldn't she leave him alone and go back to LA? He was clear about his stance on the subject, but she refused to listen. Pressure in his chest built at every click of her heels. This couldn't be healthy. He rolled his head from side to side, forcing himself to stay calm. He would not be a jerk, but one way or another, she had to know he was serious about his new life.

He stopped, then whirled around. "Look, Estelle. I've told you, I am *not* going to hold a press conference stating we are back together. It's absurd and embarrassing. No one would hold a press conference for that."

She bit her bottom lip and looked at the paved driveway. A moment later the light returned to her eyes. "Okay, you're right about announcing we're back together. I'll stand by your side as you tell the world about your new album."

"What new album?" She'd officially lost her mind.

"The one you're going to make as soon as you return to Los Angeles."

"Not happening. I don't want that life anymore and I want to be here for my mom. I can't cut a new album without losing what I have here." He glowered at her.

She blinked rapidly, and a pout covered her lips. "I don't understand why. Why would you choose living with your mother in this small town over your fabulous career? You do realize no one walks away from what you had… have. I've been here awhile now, and I don't see what the draw is."

Derek crossed his arms and studied Estelle. She was a beautiful woman who knew her way around the entertainment industry, and what she said was true, but his heart wasn't in it any longer. Why couldn't she accept that? He understood why Jerry hoped to lure him back, since he received a cut of everything Derek earned, but why did he matter so much to Estelle?

"Are you listening to me, Derek?" Her eyes flashed as she rested her hands on her hips.

"How could I not hear your incessant nagging? You're the one not listening. I left that life behind. I'm done. Finished. I'm making a life for myself here. If you need proof, look at my involvement with the Spring Festival."

She fisted her hands straight by her sides, stomped her foot and spun around. "You're going to regret this, DJ."

A sick feeling gripped Derek's stomach. What was this woman up to now? Everyone in the biz knew she had mastered the art of revenge. He'd always felt sorry for anyone on the other end of her wrath, but he'd never imagined she'd turn on him.

When he'd found out she'd been sleeping around while they were supposedly dating exclusively, it had hurt. Then *she* dumped him before he could dump her. At the time he was miffed, but in retrospect she'd done him a favor. She'd saved face, and he hadn't been dragged through the mud. By the sound of it, that was about to change. Not that it would matter. She couldn't hurt him, since he had no interest in returning to his former life.

What he'd seen in her escaped him now. But she could actually be a nice person when she wasn't caught up with landing her next acting gig and making money.

He'd been praying a lot since Estelle's arrival and felt God directing him to take the worship leader position, but how would that work now that Estelle was up to no good? Would she interfere and mess up that part of his life, too?

The only thing he could do was lay it all out there for Pastor Miller and let him decide if he was still interested. They'd spoken on the phone before Estelle showed up, but the pastor might see things differently now. He went into the house and found his mother in the kitchen.

"Where's Estelle?"

"Her room. Did you…fight?"

He didn't want to concern her with his problems, but maybe she should know what her guest was capable of. "We had words. Listen, Mom. Estelle isn't all that she seems. You need to be very careful what you say to her."

Mom chuckled. "Not saying anything that will cause a problem," she said slowly but without pauses. Although her speech was improving, the slow speed tried his patience when it was already stretched thin.

He grinned in spite of the circumstances. "What do you say we show our guest to the door?"

Mom frowned. "Whatever you think is best, but I've been sharing the Lord with her. I feel strongly I should witness to her and tell her Jesus loves her." It took her a bit to get the entire speech out, but he wasn't surprised she'd been witnessing.

"That's great, but I think it may be falling on deaf ears. I'd like her to leave."

"Okay." Her shoulders sagged, and the light in her eyes dimmed.

Was he making a mistake? Did Estelle's being there mean that much to Mom? He knew in his heart what God would say, but even though he knew it was the right thing to do, it was a tough decision.

He ground his teeth. "I need to take a drive and think. Don't say anything about this to Estelle."

He hopped into his pickup and drove to the street near the fountain where he and Kayla had kissed. He parked and sat there with his hands resting on the steering wheel. He'd love to rewind his life to that night and tell Kayla about his music career. If he'd been up-front to begin with, she probably wouldn't have been acting so put out now.

Then again, maybe it wouldn't have mattered. She seemed convinced he would return to his old life. Taking the job at the church ought to prove to her that he was here to stay. He got out and strolled up First Avenue until he came to the old white church building with the towering steeple.

A sign indicated that the church office was located in the basement and an arrow directed visitors to the rear of the building. He squared his shoulders and walked along the side of the church. Steam rose from the parking lot as the sun beat down on the wet asphalt. He rounded the corner and found stairs leading down.

"Here goes nothing." He pulled the glass door open and stepped inside. A counter straight ahead blocked all access to the doors beyond.

A smiling woman stood. "Hello, may I help you?"

"I was hoping to speak with Pastor Miller. Is he available?"

"Let me check." She stepped over to a closed white door only feet from her work area and knocked.

The pastor's deep voice rumbled, and she went in. A moment later Pastor Miller popped his head out. "Derek, great to see you. Come on back." He motioned toward a door next to the counter.

Derek followed his instructions and found himself whisked into the pastor's office. The receptionist closed the door softly behind her.

"I'm glad you stopped in. Have a seat."

Derek sat down and looked around the space. The cozy room had only one small window, which looked onto the parking lot. If anyone had been outside the window, they would have been able to see only people's feet as they walked past. He tried to ignore the closed-in feeling the room evoked by focusing his attention on the man seated before him.

Pastor Miller's round face and bald head reminded him of his dad—a good memory. He wore a gray sweater-vest over a long-sleeve button-up shirt that did little to hide his paunch. The smile he wore was the real deal. Not the fake ones he'd been getting from Estelle.

"How are you, Derek?"

"Fine."

"I spoke with your mother yesterday. She's sounding a lot better."

Derek grinned. "Yes. She's improving a lot now that she has a houseguest. I guess it's motivation to work harder." At least Estelle's presence had brought about one positive thing.

"I heard about that guest." He raised a brow as if to ask

for an explanation. "But I imagine you didn't stop in to talk about Estelle Rogers."

Though tempted to share his trouble with the pastor, he decided against it for now. "I'm here about the position. I'm sorry it's taken me so long to stop in. My life has been…nuts."

Pastor chuckled. "So I've heard, but don't worry. I have a good feeling about you."

A comforting balm washed over Derek, and he breathed easier. "How about you tell me what your expectations are?"

"Sure. You'll work with me to come up with a list of songs. There's a worship band in place—we are only missing a leader. I've been doing it for months, and to be blunt, it's not my calling."

Derek grinned. He'd heard Pastor sing and it *really* wasn't his thing.

"If I may ask, why the change of heart about leading worship? Your mom originally told me that you weren't open to the idea. I was so surprised by your phone call I forgot to ask what changed your mind. By the way, I was pleasantly surprised to hear from you."

"Thanks. Sorry it's taken me so long to get in here to talk in person. For the record, I never said I wasn't interested, but I didn't know how it could work. Actually, I'm still not sure it will work considering that I've been outed as DJ Parker."

The pastor smiled. "I've heard, which makes me wonder all the more why we are having this conversation."

Derek swallowed the lump in his throat. How could he tell the truth without sounding shallow? "Here's the deal. I don't want to continue on the path my professional music career was taking me on. I came here because I wanted to leave it all behind. Unfortunately, it caught up to me."

"In the form of Estelle Rogers?" Pastor raised an eyebrow.

"Yes. She refuses to leave town unless I agree to accompany her to Los Angeles. Which puts a serious crimp in my life and my love life, or lack thereof."

"I assume you are referring to Kayla Russell."

Derek nodded. "You really *are* in the know."

"You were spotted together on several occasions. I put two and two together. I imagine having Estelle at your mother's house isn't helping, either. I'm curious about something."

"What don't you know?"

"Why you decided to say yes."

"Leading worship is a dream of mine from way back, but I got sidetracked. I've been praying about it and feel this is what the Lord wants for me. To be completely honest, there's another reason as well, and it's not very spiritual. Kayla thinks I'm going to leave town. This is the best way to prove to her that I'm here to stay."

"I see." Pastor's face was unreadable. Had he said too much?

"I only have one concern." He waited until Pastor Miller made eye contact. "Are you sure about *me* leading worship? I tend to create a circus atmosphere."

"I'm not worried. I trust the people of this church to behave themselves. Tell you what—you can start this Sunday. Let's do a one-month trial. If at that time either of us is dissatisfied, I'll find a replacement for you. Deal?" He rose and held out his hand.

Derek's stomach leaped. He bolted to a stand and grasped the outstretched offering. "Deal."

Kayla slid her key from the lock of the flower shop with a sigh of relief. She'd made it through one more day at the store. The added responsibility of the festival along with her normal job made her wish she'd taken that vacation Jill had suggested. At least she had her part of the festival planning complete and now all that needed to be done was the float. Derek seemed convinced he would have it finished in time, and rather than worry about it, she decided to trust him—at least where the float was concerned.

Too tired to cook dinner, she headed toward the Deli on the Rye.

"Kayla!"

She stopped and looked around for the familiar voice and spotted Derek waving from across the street. Her heart skipped, and she waved back. It was difficult to stay angry with the man. He couldn't help his past, and he *was* doing her a huge favor by building the float. It was time to move past her disappointment that he wasn't the one and treat him as she'd treat any other good friend. "Hi," she called out.

"Hold on. I'll be right there." He looked both ways, then stepped into the road after a car passed and jogged across. "I have news."

His face practically glowed. She steeled herself for the news she expected to hear when she found out his true identity—he was leaving.

"I was offered a position as the worship leader at Oak Knoll Community Church."

"Isn't that kind of a step down from being a famous musician?" She scooted closer to the building to allow a mother and her children to pass.

"Not the way I see it. I've been fortunate enough to have followed *both* of my dreams."

Kayla shook her head. "You lost me."

"Where are you headed?"

"The deli." She gestured at the restaurant nearby.

"How about we grab a bite, and I'll fill you in on the details?"

She hesitated. Her gut response said no, but that was not how a friend behaved. "Sure. I'm not in any hurry."

He pushed the door open. "After you."

"Thanks." They placed their orders, then found a table. "You said you followed both of your dreams."

"Right. When I was a young teen, I felt called to the ministry as a worship pastor, but then the chance of a lifetime was handed to me, and I went in a different direction."

"I had no idea. Then again, how would I? It's not like I was a groupie."

He chuckled. "You are nothing like a groupie. Besides, that bit of information was between the Lord, me and my parents."

"Are you sure you're up to being out of the spotlight for good?" Although he seemed sincere, she couldn't help doubting he'd actually be content as a worship pastor. "You won't be traveling or singing in a different venue every night."

"I'm thankful for the experience I had and that I was so successful, but I'm through with that life." A thoughtful expression covered his face. "Tell me, what is it about me that makes it impossible to convince you that I'm not returning to my singing career?"

Kayla blinked. "Uh—"

Nick, the owner of the deli, placed two plastic baskets that held their meals on the table. "Bon appétit."

Kayla waited until Nick was out of hearing range, then cleared her throat. "I guess I'm questioning you because I would have a difficult time leaving fame and fortune behind, so I expect that you would, too."

He shrugged. "But I'm not you." He bowed his head.

Kayla followed his lead and prayed a silent blessing

over her meal. They looked up at the same time. Her gaze rested on his kind eyes. Was she making a mistake shutting her heart to him? He was as close as any man had ever come to meeting all the requirements on her list. But the one thing he lacked was a big one—she couldn't trust him. There were too many unknowns where he was concerned.

"Why do I have the feeling I've failed some kind of test?" Derek's brows furrowed as he bit into his Reuben sandwich.

Kayla shrugged. "Beats me. I've always wanted to travel. Someday I want to go to Venice and ride in a gondola."

He chuckled. "That was a rough transition. I take it you don't care to answer my question."

Her cheeks burned. She'd hoped to change subjects without him noticing.

"Don't worry—I don't mind. You'd love Venice. Would you believe I spent five months in Italy this past year?"

Her eyes widened. "No way. I'm officially jealous. I have wanted to go there for as long as I can remember."

"Do you have a passport?"

"Yes." She thought about the little blue book sitting in her dresser drawer that contained no stamps. She hadn't even been to Canada, which was an easy drive. Maybe that was where she should take the vacation Jill encouraged her to go on.

"Then why not go?"

"Venice is meant to be enjoyed with someone else." She bit into her ham and cheese on rye. She couldn't tell Derek about her silly girlhood dream of visiting Venice on her honeymoon. Going there alone would spoil the dream.

"I don't agree. I went to Italy alone and enjoyed myself a lot. Granted, I was running from everything and everyone and all I wanted was peace and solitude."

"Did you find it there?"

"For the most part." He took another huge bite and chewed slowly.

Kayla wondered what it would be like to walk the cobbled streets of the ancient city and visit the famed Saint Mark's Square. "What was your favorite part of Italy?"

"That's easy—the food." He grinned and tossed the last bite of his sandwich into his mouth.

"You were going to tell me about the details of your dream?"

"Right." He wiped his hands on a napkin. "The church position is on a one-month trial basis. If Pastor Miller or I feel it's not a good fit, I walk away."

That was exactly what she feared would happen. "Are you concerned about drawing the paparazzi into the church?"

"No. They won't go in there. I was more concerned with being a distraction and taking away from worship."

She nodded. "I can see why you'd have that concern, but that's not for you to worry about. You have no control over people and where their minds are at church."

He grinned. "Great point." He tilted his head. "What's different? You're being nicer."

She chuckled. "Yeah, sorry about the way I acted before." She reached for her cup of water and gulped down a few swallows, then set the cup down slowly. "I realized I was being silly. You had a right to keep your past private. Although I'm not sure how you expected that secret to stay hidden forever. It's not like we are on another planet." She shook her head. "Sorry, I didn't mean to sound rude. It's just that—"

He reached across the table and grasped her hand. "Relax. I think I understand. You didn't like that I deceived you and didn't get why I wasn't up-front about my past, since it was bound to come out eventually."

"Pretty much." The feel of his touch sent tingles rippling up her arm. Derek might think he was sticking around, but time would tell. How much time would pass before she was convinced he was staying? What if she waited too long, and he found someone else?

Chapter 10

Kayla waited in the foyer of the church a few feet from Derek as a couple of women a year or so younger than her fawned over him. She'd gone to high school with these ladies, and their behavior knotted her stomach. From the strained look on Derek's face, he was desperate to escape.

Surely he was used to this kind of thing, but she couldn't bear to see him so uncomfortable. She marched up to the threesome. "Hey, girls. How's it going?" She offered her best smile and motioned for Derek to make a run for it.

"If you ladies will excuse me." Without waiting for a reply, Derek fled across the foyer and down the stairs leading to the church office.

She returned her attention to the women. "That was a great service."

"Uh-huh," the duo said in unison.

Kayla pointed. "Oh, look, my mom is waving for me to hurry. She likes to get to the restaurant before the church across town lets out. See you." She hustled through the foyer and caught up with her mother at the doors leading to the sidewalk. They'd walk to Bridget's Diner since it was only a block away.

"Your Derek did a fine job this morning," Mom said as she clipped along beside Kayla. "I heard a lot of folks talking and they were pleasantly surprised."

"About what?" She'd let it go that Mom called him *her* Derek since even though it wasn't a reality, she'd like to secretly think of him as hers.

"Some of them doubted his ability to lead worship, but I must say he did well."

Kayla's insides warmed, and she walked with a little bounce in her step. "I agree. I'm afraid I was one of those doubters, too, but not anymore. I'm really proud of him."

"I have a surprise for you at the diner."

A smile touched her lips. She loved surprises, and her mom's were always good. "What is it?"

Mom dragged a finger across her lips; then she mimed locking them and tossing the imaginary key.

"Not even a hint?" Several people milled around outside Bridget's. Hadn't her church service gotten out on time? She glanced at her cell phone and gasped. "We're ten minutes late!"

"No worries. I sent someone ahead to get us a table." Mom's eyes gleamed mischief.

Kayla's insides trilled in anticipation of the surprise. She pulled the door open, motioned for her mom to go in first and followed.

Mom greeted the hostess, then strode toward the back dining room, where it was generally a little quieter. Bridget's Diner had been a staple in Oak Knoll for as long as she could remember and they'd been having Sunday lunch here for years. Mom stopped beside a booth where a handsome man sat. With his trim physique, tanned skin, and salt-and-pepper hair, he reminded her of George Clooney.

He grinned wide, flashing his perfect teeth, and stood. "I was beginning to wonder what happened to you." He pulled Mom into a hug and kissed her cheek.

"Close your mouth, dear," Mom said as she scooted into the booth. "Stan, this is my daughter, Kayla. Kayla, meet Stan."

Kayla tipped her head to the side—*the* Stan from Florida? Why was he here, and why did she have a feeling life had just taken a crazy twist?

"Your mother has told me so much about you." He slid in beside Mom.

Kayla gave a tentative smile as she sat across from the couple and worked to form an intelligent thought. "She said she had a surprise waiting, but I never imagined it would be you. It's nice to meet you, Stan. Where are you staying?"

"The Best Western."

"Oh." She'd half expected he'd be staying in her guestroom, but then, maybe her mom didn't feel comfortable with that arrangement. It *was* Kayla's house, after all.

"Stan flew into Portland on Friday."

"So you've been in town a couple of days, and my mom is just now getting around to introducing us?" She raised a brow and sent her mother a you-have-some-explaining-to-do look.

Mom's face glowed and she seemed clueless to Kayla's tease. She looked at Stan with such love in her eyes. What was really going on here? Kayla narrowed her eyes, and then she saw it. Her mom's left-hand ring finger held a rock she had to be blind not to have seen.

"You're engaged? Oh my goodness!"

Mom nodded and held out her hand for Kayla to examine the ring.

"You sure didn't waste any time. Congratulations!" Excitement tempered with caution bubbled through her. Her mom deserved to find love again, but she and Stan barely knew each other. How could they possibly jump into marriage so quickly?

Stan chuckled. "When it's right, it's right." He looked to her mother and cradled her hand between his.

Mom's eyes shone with adoration.

How had she missed that her mother was so much in love? She *had* been distracted since Derek walked into the flower shop last month.

"Are you okay, sweetie?" Mom's forehead scrunched. "I'm sorry for springing this on you. I didn't think—"

"I'm fine. I'm sorry I was so caught up in my own drama that I missed yours."

"You've been focused elsewhere lately, what with the festival preparations and mooning over Derek."

"I wasn't mooning." Kayla cast a quick glance at Stan. A knowing smile covered his face. "I was… Oh, I don't know what I was doing, but it wasn't mooning."

Stan chuckled again. "She's exactly like you described her, Livy."

Mom nodded.

Livy? No one had ever been allowed to shorten Mom's name. She'd always demanded that everyone call her Olivia. Clearly her mother was in love, but marriage? Kayla looked down and realized she was shredding her paper napkin, but she really was happy for them, and Stan seemed like a kind man who clearly loved her mother, but still… They'd known one another for only a couple of months.

Derek's baby blues danced in her mind, sending her heart into overdrive. So what if she'd known him a few days before tossing around the idea of marrying him? Besides, she hadn't followed that train of thought all the way to the station. "When is the wedding?"

Mom and Stan glanced at each other. His face sobered. "We still need to tell my children, and I'm not sure they'll take it as well as you."

Kayla gulped. She'd been an only child her entire life, and now she would have three stepsiblings. But they were all adults, so they'd probably never see each other except at holiday gatherings. Her gaze darted toward the exit. She needed time to digest this news away from her mother. Mom knew her too well and would sense her unease. "How about you lovebirds take lunch to figure things out? I can grab a bite to eat at home."

"Are you sure, honey?"

"Yes. I'll catch up with you later. And, Stan, don't be a stranger. I expect to see you at our place for dinner every night you're in town. That is, unless you have other plans." She scooted out and stood, not waiting for a reply.

On the way to the exit, she bumped shoulders with a man. "Excuse me," she mumbled, and kept going.

"Kayla?"

She looked up and started—Derek.

Derek studied Kayla's pale face. "You okay?"

"I'm fine, but if you plan on eating here, you're going to stay hungry for a while. They're packed." She pressed her lips together. "You have to get here early to get a table on Sundays."

"Now you tell me," he said playfully. He'd planned to meet his mom here. Estelle was supposed to drop her off, but she'd just sent a text saying his mother had been cleaning the house all morning and was taking a nap instead.

He'd been on his way out when Kayla had rammed into him. "Have you eaten?"

She shook her head.

He grinned. "In that case, let's get out of here. I have an idea."

"I don't know, Derek. I feel a headache coming on."

Her face registered turmoil. What was going on? He gently guided her out the door into the cool sunny day—the perfect spring afternoon.

"What a relief to be out of there." She rubbed her palm on her forehead. "I skipped breakfast."

"Is that why you have a headache?"

"Probably. That and the fact my mom and her fiancé just announced their engagement."

He let out a low whistle. "We've both had quite a day. How about grabbing takeout and eating in the park?"

She looked around. "Where's your entourage?"

"I think they gave up and returned to Los Angeles. Estelle never leaves the house, although she was going to drop my mom at Bridget's Diner. She must have lain low long enough the paparazzi figured she'd gone home."

"So she's still here?"

Was that censure in her eyes? He probably deserved it, but after talking with Pastor Miller the other day and praying, he felt it was best to let his mom decide when it was time to send Estelle packing.

"She's a guest of my mother at this point, or I'd have sent her away a long time ago. My mom seems to enjoy her company, and she feels strongly that she needs to share the Lord with Estelle. After all Mom has been through, I don't want to upset her." He shrugged. "It's her house. I'm staying in the guest cottage out back."

"Okay."

"Okay to get food or okay about Estelle?"

"Both." She grabbed his arm. "Come on. I'm starving and food will probably help ease this headache." She tossed him a grin as they set out on foot.

"Where are we going? Not Deli on the Rye, I hope. I'm getting burned-out on sandwiches."

"We're headed to the church to get my car."

"Hmm. Someplace we need to drive to. Intriguing." This playful side of Kayla intrigued him. "I can drive my rig."

She chuckled. "I'd never be able climb into your pickup with this skirt."

He admired her fitted black skirt and red heels. "Okay, I see your point." He spotted her car in the church parking lot, and within minutes she'd whisked them off to the other side of town where a food cart sat on the side of the road. "I didn't know Oak Knoll had food carts."

"This one only comes to town on Sundays. I discovered it when my mom was in Florida. They make the best pulled-pork barbecue you'll ever taste. Trust me when I say order the special."

"Two specials, please." He had no idea what it was, but he trusted Kayla's advice. He withdrew his wallet and paid.

"I can get my own."

"No way. Not after you saved me from those women at church this morning."

She grinned. "They were harmless."

"To you, maybe, but not me," he said with a dramatic flair.

He took a large bag that seemed rather heavy for only two meals, and Kayla grabbed the giant drink cups filled with lemonade. "Where to now?"

She pointed across the street to a neatly manicured grassy knoll that looked onto a pond half-covered with lily pads. "There are a few benches and picnic tables." They strolled across the road side by side. "I can't believe we get this place to ourselves. Maybe there's something to eating after the lunch rush."

"This is normally a busy spot?" He placed their bag on a large wooden picnic table.

"On nice days like today, yes." They sat and Kayla pulled out two foil-wrapped packages and handed him one.

As he unfolded the wrapper, steam billowed out, carrying the barbecue aroma straight to his taste buds. He blessed the food for them, then dug in. Flavor exploded in his mouth. She hadn't been kidding that this sandwich would be the best he'd ever tasted. He didn't even mind that it was a sandwich.

Kayla caught his attention and pointed to her chin.

He reached for a napkin and wiped the dripping sauce. "Thanks. How do you feel about your mom remarrying?"

"I'm happy she's happy. They both look very much in love."

"But?" He suspected there was more, or she wouldn't have been in such a hurry to escape the restaurant earlier.

"I'm worried they're rushing. Stan has three grown children, and apparently he doesn't expect them to welcome my mom, and that *really* bothers me. And then I thought about family gatherings and realized I may have to deal with hostile stepsiblings. I've never even had a sibling. It's a lot to process."

"I didn't know you're an only child. I am, too."

"How would you handle the situation if it were you?"

"I'd buy them all trips to Italy, and they'd adore me for life." He took another bite.

She shook her head. "Be serious. What would you do?"

He swallowed and sobered. "I don't know, Kayla. It's

difficult to see myself in that situation, considering my mom's health issues."

She frowned. "Sorry." A little sauce clung to the side of her mouth.

He wanted to kiss it away but instead reached across the table and gently wiped it away. Her eyes widened and locked on his. "Sauce."

She cleared her throat. "Thanks. Have you noticed how often we eat together?"

He hadn't until she mentioned it. "Why do you suppose that is?"

"I don't like to cook and neither do you." She propped her elbows on the table and rested her chin on her laced fingers.

"Ah, I learned another thing about you. You don't cook."

"I didn't say I don't cook. I don't *enjoy* cooking, so I eat out often."

He dipped his chin. "You want to walk?"

"I'd love to, but these shoes weren't made for walking, and I've already done more than my feet appreciate."

"Okay, let's just sit and talk some more." He racked his mind for a safe topic. "The float is ready to be painted."

Her face lit. "That's great news. Why didn't you say something sooner?"

"I forgot."

"Can I see it today?" Excitement danced in her eyes.

"Sure. Let's go." Would she like the extra something he'd included that wasn't in the original design?

Chapter 11

Monday evening after work, with paint roller in hand, Kayla rested her knees on the float and carefully applied primer to one end of the bridge while Derek worked toward her from the opposite end. Jill and Charlie worked on the arbor near the front. Jill's laughter brought a smile to Kayla's face.

Derek's surprise had turned out to be a swing attached to the arbor rather than the simple bench. Whoever rode the float would get to sit there. They were holding a drawing at the shop to see which lucky citizen would get to ride the float. She almost wanted to do it herself, but she'd be way too busy with other things.

Contentment settled on her. This was the life. Sunshine beat down on her back, increasing her pleasure. "I had no idea painting could be so relaxing." Kayla shot a grin toward Derek.

"When you're with friends, and it's not detail work—

it's fun. But tedious painting is not for me." Derek loaded his roller.

"I'll be sure to get someone else to paint the tedious spots. I can't thank you enough for designing and building this." Kayla would have to think of a way to thank him, but later. Right now she was enjoying the company and the unseasonably warm weather. Spring had taken a leap toward summer. The thermometer in her car read seventy-five degrees on her way over, and she loved the warmth.

"It's been fun." He flashed a grin before returning his attention to the bridge. "It was a nice change of pace to use my hands in a creative way."

Kayla tipped her head to the side. "I imagine your life as a singer didn't lend itself to this kind of thing."

"Nope. But change is in the air."

Kayla studied his profile in the dim light. Was he trying to tell her he'd decided to return to LA? Or was he suggesting something else?

"I heard worship went well yesterday, Derek," Jill said. "I'm sorry I wasn't there. It was my Sunday to volunteer in the children's service."

"You didn't miss much," he shot back.

"Don't let him kid you, Jill." Kayla reloaded her roller. "The spirit of the Lord was in that room yesterday, and I don't think one person there thought twice about the fact that DJ Parker was leading them." Somehow even she'd managed to forget he was a famous singer and enter into worship.

Derek stared at her as if in disbelief. "Are you kidding me? Clearly you were sitting in the front, or you would have seen something completely different."

"Huh?" Kayla stilled. "What are you talking about?" The only comments she'd heard had been positive.

"Those women you rescued me from after church had

their cell phones out and were waving them in the air during worship."

Her jaw dropped, and she snapped it shut. "Please tell me you're kidding."

Charlie chuckled. "'Fraid not. I saw them, too."

Kayla shot him a look. "I didn't know you attended Oak Knoll Community."

"I don't normally, but a certain lady invited me to visit, then ditched me for the children's service."

"Oh no! Jill, you should have said something. I'd have filled in for you."

Jill whipped the paintbrush in the air and flicked white paint that landed a foot from Kayla. "Oops, sorry about that."

Kayla took a rag and wiped up the paint. Maybe no one would see the splotch, but she wanted the float to be as close to perfect as possible.

Jill sent Charlie an exasperated look. "I didn't *know* he would be there, or I would have asked you to step in."

Kayla pressed her lips together. Was there trouble in paradise already? She studied her friends—the two looked as smitten with one another as ever. The momentary concern evaporated. "So other than Mary and Bethany's odd behavior, did the rest of worship go well from your perspective, Derek?"

"I suppose so. I did my best to block them out, but it was hard."

She shook her head. "I don't know what got into those two. They aren't like that normally." Was that the kind of thing Derek had dealt with during his career? Of course it was, because that was what people did at concerts, but *not* during church. "I wonder if someone should speak with them."

"I believe Pastor Miller was going to have a gentle talk

with the ladies." Derek ducked his head and rolled paint over the last of his side of the bridge. "Better him than my mom. When I told her about it, you should have heard her." He chuckled.

"Speaking of moms, Kayla, I heard your mom is engaged," Jill said. "When's the big day?"

Stan had stopped in last night, and she'd enjoyed getting to know him. She could understand why her mom had fallen for him. He was a kind and considerate man who put others before himself. "They haven't set a date, but I have a strong feeling they want to get married as soon as possible. My mom is flying out with Stan on Friday to meet his children. He's invited them to his place for the weekend."

"Are you going?" Charlie asked.

She shuddered. "No." Meeting her future stepsiblings under those circumstances would not be good. "Call me a coward—I don't care—but I'd rather get to know them when they aren't in shock or angry that their dad is remarrying."

Derek looked at her sympathetically. "You're not a coward. You're smart."

Her heart thrilled at his words. "Thanks." His kindness along with everything else made it difficult not to fall for him. She steeled herself against his charm, but it wasn't easy when everyone around her was finding love. Being content to stick to her list had been much simpler when those closest to her were single. Now it bothered her a lot that she couldn't find someone who matched all the qualifications on her list. Granted, Derek came closer than any man ever had; however, he wasn't an option. Then again, maybe he was? He really seemed to be putting roots down in Oak Knoll.

The screen door on the house slammed. "Hi, everyone."

Estelle stood on the porch holding a tray with a pitcher and cups. For once a genuine smile lit her eyes. "I made lemonade and Helen made sugar cookies." She sat on the top stair and rested the tray on her lap. "Come and get it."

Kayla stifled a groan. Right when everything was going so well, *she* had to make an appearance. Her stomach twisted as guilt for her harsh feelings toward the woman ate at her. Estelle might not be the kind of person Kayla had thought she was, but she didn't have to treat the star with disdain. Especially since she was making an effort to be kind. "Thanks, Estelle. That was nice of you to bring those out for us. How about we all take a break?"

Derek narrowed his eyes. "Just a quick one. We don't want the paint to dry on the brushes and rollers."

"What a taskmaster." Kayla rolled her eyes and playfully punched his shoulder. "No wonder you are so successful at everything you do." She might have been teasing him, but there was an element of truth to her words. The man worked hard and put everything into whatever he did. She admired that quality.

He hopped off the end of the float and offered her a hand. She placed her fingers in his palm and stepped down. "Don't let her fool you, Kayla," he said softly into her ear. "Estelle never does anything without an ulterior motive. She's up to something, so be careful."

Kayla turned startled eyes toward him. Clearly the two had history, but she'd never taken him for being bitter. "Thanks for the warning, but I think she may just be trying to fit in with your friends."

Derek eyed Estelle with suspicion as she handed him a cup of cold lemonade. Maybe Kayla was right about Estelle, but he wouldn't let his guard down so easily. Her warning about him regretting crossing her never strayed far from his mind.

Jill, Charlie and Kayla all took cookies and drinks, then sat in the shade on the porch.

"So when is this festival I keep hearing so much about?" Estelle crossed her legs at her ankles.

"April twenty-ninth." Kayla sipped from the cup and smiled. "This tastes like fresh-squeezed lemonade."

"It is." Estelle dipped her chin. "Do you like it?"

Kayla nodded. "It's perfect. Will you be here for the festival, Estelle?"

Derek's gaze shot to Estelle's.

"Maybe. I don't have any firm plans."

Surely she wouldn't be here that long? Derek's pulse ramped up. When his mom asked that he allow Estelle to continue to stay, he'd never imagined she'd still be here. Regret for not insisting his mom send her packing threatened to overwhelm him.

Lord, what is going on here? I felt like You directed me to leave this up to my mom, but now I'm not sure.

Peace settled over him and his pulse slowed. *Okay. I understand You are in control of this. Please help, though, because I don't like this—at all.*

Charlie got up and said, "Thanks for the snack, Estelle, but we'd better get back to painting."

Estelle didn't even bother to look at Charlie. She kept her cold eyes focused on Derek and stood with the tray. Without a word, she pivoted and sashayed inside.

Derek rubbed the back of his neck. "Well, that was awkward."

Jill laughed softly as she ambled past him. "Don't worry about her, Derek. She'll go home sooner or later. It was nice of her to bake for us."

"I hope she leaves sooner rather than later, cookies or

not," he mumbled as he copied Charlie and tossed his ice into the planter.

"Derek. Come quick!" Estelle's piercing yell ripped through the air.

Mom! His heart kicked into double time, and he charged up the stairs and into the house. "Where are you? Mom?" He ran into the kitchen and spotted his mother lying on the tile floor, pushing against Estelle, who seemed to be trying to keep her prone.

He rushed to her side. "Mom, what happened?"

"I slipped and knocked my head. I'm fine, other than this pounding headache."

"Do you think you can get up?" Derek asked.

Mom gave Estelle a patient smile. "If you would give me a hand, I'm sure I'll be fine."

Estelle bit her lower lip and shot him a concerned look. His heart softened toward her slightly. She couldn't be all bad if she cared this much for his mother. "Do you hurt anywhere besides your head?"

"My hips and back hurt, but I'm sure I'm fine. It's not like I'm a frail old woman. I just slipped on a wet spot."

"Okay. How about you sit up nice and slow?" He'd heard once that when someone fell, it was best not to help her get up. Something about if the person could stand on her own, then she was fine, but if not, you could risk injuring her further. However, he offered her a hand to pull her up so she could sit.

Mom sat there for a moment with closed eyes. "A little light-headed."

He swallowed the lump that had formed in his throat.

Her eyes blinked open. "Okay. I'm better now." She used one arm to push up to standing and swayed.

Derek caught her and scooped her into his arms. "I'm taking you to Emergency."

"I don't think that's necessary."

"Just the same. I want to have your head checked for a concussion."

"He's right, Helen." Estelle brushed a curl from Mom's face. "You should get checked out. I'll even go with you." She offered a sweet smile.

"You're a nice young woman, but I know what going out in public is like for you. I want you to stay here. My son can take me." Her words, though slow, were clear.

Although his mom was light for a five-foot-five woman, his arms were beginning to shake.

"Allow me." Charlie's bulky frame filled the entrance to the kitchen.

"I can walk," Mom snapped.

Shocked to obedience, Derek set her down. "Okay. Sorry." She *never* snapped. Mom was one of the most patient people he'd ever known.

She looped her hand around his arm. "If we must do this, let's get a move on. It's getting late."

"Yes, ma'am." He kept his gait slow.

Charlie stepped out of the way, and Derek spotted Jill and Kayla behind him, both wearing worried expressions.

"I'm going to run her to the hospital."

"Would you like one of us to keep you company?" Kayla asked.

He started to shake his head, but Mom interrupted.

"That would be lovely, Kayla."

"I need to run home and change and then I'll meet you there." She spun around and bolted for the door.

Charlie kept his voice low. "Don't worry about anything here. Jill and I will clean up."

"Thanks." He wondered at his mom's acceptance of Kayla's offer but kept his thoughts to himself as he helped his mother climb into his pickup.

Fifteen minutes later he pulled into the hospital's parking lot and parked. "How you doing, Mom?" She hadn't spoken once since they'd left her house.

"I'm alive. Let's get this over with." She pushed open the door and slid out before he could assist.

He ran around and offered his arm as they walked inside.

"I hate this place," Mom grumbled.

He raised a brow but remained silent as he guided her to the check-in counter. It wasn't long before Kayla rushed in. Her face lit when her gaze landed on them. She looked good. Her jeans fit perfectly, and the sleeveless teal-blue blouse she wore complemented her fair complexion.

She strode over to them and sat across from him. "Did they say how long she'd have to wait?"

He shook his head. "But they don't seem to be overly busy." Just then his mom's name was called. "Would you like me to go with you?"

"No." Mom stood and walked away, disappearing behind sliding doors.

"Thanks for coming to wait with me." He ached to take her hand but refrained.

"What happened, anyway?" Kayla moved over and sat beside him.

He explained what he knew, then closed his eyes and prayed. Kayla might not realize it, but her presence calmed him. He thanked the Lord she'd come to wait with him, and then he asked for healing for his mom. She'd been through a lot lately, and there was only so much one body could take. He opened his eyes.

"I'm glad you were still in town when your mom fell. Otherwise, who knows what would've happened? Can I get you anything?" Kayla asked. "Water, a mocha…" Her gaze held concern.

"I'm fine, and thanks for coming."

"That's what friends are for."

Friends. He wanted to be so much more than that, but that opportunity had passed. Or had it?

Chapter 12

Derek sat on a stool in the church sanctuary holding his guitar. This Sunday's song list sat nearly blank on the music stand in front of him. It was only Tuesday, and he had until tomorrow to turn the list in to Pastor Miller, but instead of working, he kept tossing around Kayla's comment. What would have happened to his mother if he hadn't been there? If he'd returned with Estelle to LA and his singing career, Mom would have been all alone when she fell. His throat thickened at the thought.

He liked the vibe of Oak Knoll, and the friends he'd made here were true, which made him all the more happy he'd come. He glanced at the clock that hung above the doors leading into the sanctuary—almost noon.

"How's it going?" Tom, the church janitor, stepped out from behind the stage.

Derek jumped. "You startled me."

"Sorry about that. I've been taken by surprise more

than once, so I tried to make noise as I climbed the stairs. I thought you'd hear me."

The wood stairs that led from the basement to the rear of the stage had no carpet, and he should have easily heard him. Derek looked down at the sheet of paper on the music stand in front of him. "It's not going well. I'm distracted. But I'll have the list to Pastor by tomorrow as he requested."

Tom dragged a chair over and sat. "Not my business, but you seem bothered. What's going on? I've seen Pastor Miller create the Sunday song list enough to know something is causing you not to have finished yet." He glanced at his watch. "You've been in here for over an hour. You had this list whipped out in no time last week."

He studied Tom. The man was probably old enough to be his dad, and his kind eyes made Derek want to trust him. "I know, and you're right. It's Kayla."

Tom nodded. "Kayla Russell?"

"Yeah. I'm crazy about her, and I can't get her out of my head, which I need to do because she wants nothing to do with me. At least romantically."

"How do you know? From what I hear, the two of you spend a lot of time together."

"We see each other because of the parade float I'm helping build, but she's very clearly not interested in me the same way I am in her." Maybe he'd be better off moving back to Los Angeles, where there were plenty of women to distract him from pining over Kayla. He tossed the horrible thought away. That life wasn't for him.

Tom frowned. "That's too bad. I think you'd be good together. I've known Kayla most of her life and music is a big part of who she is. I figured that's why the two of you connected so well. Did you know she was runner-up in the Miss Oregon Teen pageant?"

Derek jerked his head in Tom's direction. "No way! I mean, she's beautiful and all, but I never pegged her for a pageant kind of girl."

"She's not. Someone nominated her, and her mom forced her to participate. As it turned out, she was a natural." He shook his head. "Unfortunately, my daughter dreamed of being Miss Oregon Teen and was so jealous of Kayla's success she shared a secret with me that she probably shouldn't have." He lowered his voice. "But it's one you might like to know, too. Has she told you about her list?"

"Uh…I don't think so." Something told him whatever Tom was talking about was significant. He set his guitar on the stand beside him, plopped down on the carpeted stage, stretched out his legs and leaned back on his elbows. "I'd like to hear about it."

"The only reason I know is my daughter and Kayla were good friends when they were younger. But like I said, in a moment of blind jealousy Lisa ranted about how perfect Kayla was and that she hoped she'd never find a guy that met all the traits on her husband list."

"Excuse me?"

Tom nodded. "I've always wondered about that list. Especially since she's still single. It must be quite a catalog of requirements." He stood. "I should probably practice what the pastor preaches and stop gossiping."

"Before you go, I'm curious about something. What was her talent in the pageant?"

"Singing." Tom left the stage the same way he'd arrived and disappeared behind the paneled door.

Kayla sang? He thought back to their first and only real date and recalled her saying she could carry a tune. It was interesting that she'd held back that information even though she hadn't known his full identity at the time. Did she still sing?

The door to the sanctuary opened, and a harried woman burst in. "Oh, good, I'm glad you're still here. The lady downstairs said she thought you might have left."

Derek got to his feet. "May I help you with something?" He walked down the steps.

"My name is Margie. I'm the coordinator of the Spring Festival, and I am hoping you can help me with a problem." The lanky woman strode to the edge of the stage and stopped. Her straight brown hair was pulled into a ponytail, and she looked as if she'd come from the gym.

"Shoot."

"I'd booked a local band for the festival, and I just heard the band broke up and now they are canceling all their appearances."

"That's rough. Don't they have a contract you can hold them to?" He hoped she wasn't here for the reason he suspected.

"I wish, but they've been our headliner for several years, and it's never seemed necessary. I'm at my wit's end. We have to have a concert to close out the festival. It's always a huge draw, and we've already sold half of the tickets."

He'd seen this kind of thing happen before, but not often. "Do you have a backup plan? Is there another local group you could contact?"

"Kind of. I was hoping you'd agree to perform."

Exactly what he feared. "I, umm…" He snapped his mouth closed. The last thing he wanted to do was draw attention to himself and bring the paparazzi back to town. He opened his mouth again to say no, but yes came out instead.

"Thank you!" She beamed a smile and thrust a sheet of paper at him.

"What's this?"

"A contract." Her voice came out small and somewhat apologetic. "I don't want a repeat of what happened."

"I'll look it over and get it back to you."

"Great." She handed him a business card. "Give me a call, and I'll stop in to pick it up." She whirled around, then speed-walked to the exit at the back of the sanctuary.

Maybe he should make a space in his mother's barn to work. He might get something accomplished with fewer interruptions. Wait until he told Kayla about this. He studied the standard and straightforward contract, then signed it and set it aside. He looked at his guitar resting in its stand, and an idea struck him that might convince Kayla to give them a second chance.

The bells on the doors at Flowers and More jangled and drew Kayla's attention.

Margie breezed in wearing a huge smile. "Girl, your man is simply wonderful. Do you know what he did?"

"No." It would do no good to correct her assumption that Derek was her man. It seemed half the town thought that.

"The band I booked for the festival broke up and canceled on us, which stinks, but it's all good because DJ Parker is stepping in. Can you believe it? We have a huge celebrity singing in our town." Margie's face beamed. "I've heard people refer to him as Derek. What does he go by?"

"Derek Wood is his real name. But you should put DJ Parker on the tickets and advertisements."

"You're right. I have a lot of work to redo." She whirled around. "Give your man a big hug from me, will you?"

Kayla lifted a hand to wave, but Margie was already out the door. "Oh my goodness. What was Derek thinking?" Her stomach knotted. He'd said he wasn't returning to his singing career, but it looked as if he couldn't leave it behind after all. What was next? Would Estelle be able to convince him to go back to LA now that he was singing again?

"I thought I heard Margie." Jill sidled up to her and looked from side to side. "Where'd she go?"

"Gone. She is beyond excited by the new headliner for the festival concert." Unease settled over Kayla. She needed to see Derek.

"But I already bought tickets to hear Gracie and the Band. I love them."

"Sorry to be the one to break the news to you, but the band broke up."

"What? No more Gracie and the Band?" She sighed. "Who is performing instead?"

"One guess."

Jill bit her bottom lip. Then a moment later her face lit. "Derek?"

Kayla nodded. "You're lucky you have a ticket. I probably should get one before they're sold out. As soon as the word gets out, they'll go fast."

Jill grabbed the phone.

"Who are you calling?"

"The chamber of commerce. I want more tickets. I'll get you one, too."

Kayla shook her head and walked away. What was it about celebrities that caused people to act out of character? She busied herself with putting merchandise that customers had placed in the wrong spots back where it belonged. If she were honest with herself, she'd admit that having Derek sing at the festival thrilled her as much as it did Margie and Jill, but it scared her, too. She didn't want to lose her friendship with him when he realized he wanted his old life back.

"Jill, would you mind watching the shop for a bit?"

"Nope. I'm all caught up with everything, and the workroom sparkles."

"Thanks." She slipped off her apron, grabbed her purse and headed to her car. She could walk, but she didn't want to be gone long. A couple of minutes later she pulled into the church parking lot. Good, Derek's truck was still here. Since he didn't have an office, she headed for the sanctuary.

The doors were closed, but guitar music filtered through. A sweet melody she didn't recognize warmed her to her toes. She closed her eyes and listened. The melody stopped and silence wrapped around her. She pulled the door open and spotted him sitting on the stairs to the platform writing something down. "That was nice. Is it for Sunday?"

His head whipped up. "No. It's something new I'm working on."

"You mean you wrote it?"

He nodded. "I'm in the zone. Can I call you later?"

Her stomach tensed. She never should have bothered him at work. "Of course. I'm sorry for interrupting." She shot him a forced smile. "Back to creating." Stepping out, she let the door close, then leaned against it. Her heart beat an uneven tempo. The man had an unhealthy effect on her. She couldn't help but wonder what kind of husband Derek would be. Would he dedicate himself to his wife, or would music always be his first love? She slunk from the building renewing her stance to keep him at arm's length—he was a friend, and she had no business getting her feelings hurt because he was too busy to talk with her.

The pep talk did little to ease the knot in her stomach. She unlocked her car and slid inside. The door to the church opened and Derek bolted out.

"Kayla, wait!" He jogged over to her car.

A tingle zipped up her body. She lowered the window.

"I wanted to explain."

"No need. I understand you're busy."

"Not too busy for a quick visit. I'm sorry for blowing you off." He ran his hands up and down his bare arms.

Kayla unlocked the doors. "Hop in." The temperature had dropped to the upper fifties and a slight breeze put a nip in the air.

He strode around the front of her car and slid in beside her. "I'm filling in for the headliner band at the festival, and I don't want to sing my old stuff. I was working on a new song."

"Wow. Now I'm doubly impressed. Anything I can do to help?" As if he would need *her* help. She had no skill when it came to writing music.

"Could you sing backup? A little birdie told me you were once quite a singer." He raised a brow. "By the way, I can't believe you never mentioned that."

Her cheeks flushed. "It's not something I generally share." She chuckled, then sobered. "It's nice of you to ask me to sing with you. I'm flattered, but you haven't even heard my voice. What if you hate it?"

"Impossible," he said softly.

The tender look in his eyes sent chills through her. "I don't know. I'm more of a shower singer now."

He looked down at his lap and quirked his head to the side. "That's too bad. I'm kind of boring all by myself."

She laughed. "I doubt that very much."

"Please give it some thought."

Pastor Miller strolled past her car and waved.

Kayla waved back. "Will you get in trouble for being out here with me?"

"Naw." He opened the door. "But I should head in and finish that song list for Sunday."

"Okay." She sucked in her bottom lip and watched him jog to the door. Could she really do what Derek wanted? She'd secretly dreamed of being a backup singer when she was younger. This could be her one and only chance.

Chapter 13

Late Friday afternoon Derek powered on the space heater he'd brought into the barn, then stood back to admire his work.

Though the room was utilitarian, it would make a sufficient recording studio thanks to acoustic panels and soundproofing.

He'd come to the conclusion that working as a worship pastor was great, but he needed more and that more was going to be composing. He'd always performed his own stuff, and for the most part his songs had been hits. Why couldn't he write for other singers? When it came down to it, music was his passion, and he couldn't completely abandon the industry.

He now had the perfect writing environment. Granted, he might eventually move out of his mom's guest cottage and find his own place, but she wasn't going anywhere. He could always come here to work and be nearby if she had any problems. Best of all, he'd made progress on the song he was writing for Kayla. He glanced at the cover sheet on the music stand. The top song, "Valentine's Day 3-6-5." Kayla's dislike of the holiday inspired the song, and he hoped it would bring a smile to her face. The melody was complete and the first verse finished. Now to write the chorus.

He sat on a tall black stool in the center of the room, strumming his Gibson and running the lyrics through his head. Twenty minutes later he had the second verse and chorus. He couldn't help imagining the shock on her face when she heard this song that was clearly for her and no one else.

Satisfied with the end result, he pulled out the list of worship songs he'd compiled for this Sunday and practiced until a knock sounded on the door. He glanced out the window and saw Kayla's car. He'd been in the zone and hadn't noticed anyone driving up.

"Just a minute," he called, and quickly hid the lyrics for her song behind the worship list. "Come in."

The door opened, and he jumped up. Kayla stood at the threshold. Her hair cascaded in soft waves to her shoulders, and her eyes gleamed mischief.

"What's going on?" He walked toward her.

She held up her hand, palm facing him. "Stay. I'll be right back."

What was the girl up to?

A moment later she strode in carrying a keyboard. "Where should I put this?"

"Uh, I have a keyboard." He pointed to the instrument beside the soundboard.

Shock registered on her face for only a second before she grinned. "You play piano, too?"

"Only chords, but that's really all I need to do."

She still stood holding her keyboard. The thing was big.

"Let me get that for you." He walked over to Kayla and relieved her of the burden.

"What should I do with it?"

"This looks like the real deal."

"It is. My parents bought it for me when I was a kid. It takes up less space than a piano and they made sure to get one with weighted and full-size keys." She motioned to the keyboard. "I guess it can go back into the trunk of my car."

He nodded and moved past her with the instrument. "You should get a case for this thing if you're going to cart it around."

She walked beside him. "I never take it out of my house. I thought since you wanted me to sing backup at the festival concert, I could hide behind my keyboard and sing."

He stopped mid-step. "You what?" He thought she was set against singing backup. His pulse increased—every song he'd written was for her, and he wanted to surprise her.

"You heard me. I decided to sing backup." She continued forward and he followed. "If I'd known this was going to be such a shock, I'd have insisted on carrying my keyboard myself. You're not going to faint on me or something, are you?"

He chuckled. "Very funny."

She popped the trunk, and he gently placed it inside. What was he going to do about Kayla? He couldn't rescind the offer for her to sing backup. Sure, he'd made it several days ago, and she'd turned him down flat, but the decision to sing couldn't have been easy for her.

She wrinkled her nose and frowned. "Wait a minute. You do still *want* a backup singer don't you?"

He shot her a grin, trying to hide his concern, and

wrapped an arm across her shoulder. "Of course, but I need to rethink my set since I wasn't planning on having you join me."

"Oh." Her shoulders slumped ever so slightly. He probably wouldn't have noticed if he hadn't had his hand resting on one. "I don't have to sing." She shrugged off his arm and stepped away from him. "I only wanted to help since you've been so helpful with the float."

"Oh, no, you don't." He took her hand and dragged her toward the barn. "You're not getting off that easy. I said I'd need to rethink the set, not that I didn't want you." He'd tossed aside one song he didn't think would work, but as a duet it would be perfect. "I have an idea." He let her into the room and gently pushed her onto the keyboard bench. "Give me a minute to dig something up."

He pulled out a file folder and flipped through the pages. The music was on the computer, but he'd printed off a copy and wanted to give it to Kayla. He'd written this for a movie a few years ago, but the producers hadn't thought it was the right fit. The song was one that had always stuck with him, but he'd never had the right partner. Maybe, just maybe, Kayla's voice would work, and she'd agree to sing a duet.

He handed her the sheet music and held his breath.

She studied the music for a minute, then looked at him with wide eyes. "This is a duet."

"It is. Before you freak out, take a listen. Jump in when you're comfortable." He picked up his guitar and started playing the song he knew so well. Two lines into it, the keyboard joined in and Kayla's rich voice blended with his. She was better than he'd imagined. They crescendoed to the chorus, and she broke off into the harmony.

He played the bridge as a solo; then their voices joined together again to the end. The song finished softly, and the vibrations from his guitar faded until silence filled the room. His eyes met Kayla's. "Wow."

Her eyes sparkled with delight. "That song is so beautiful. When did you find the time to write it?"

"It's from a few years back. I wasn't planning to use it, but I'd like to close with it, if you don't mind. I have several fun upbeat songs planned for the start. Since you said you didn't want to sing with me, I, umm…" How did he tell her he didn't want her to join him until the end without hurting her feelings?

"You don't want a backup singer after all?"

He shook his head. "I wrote all new stuff for this gig, and I think it would be best if I go solo until the end. I think the addition of our duet will be the perfect ending." He studied her face, hoping to read something in it about her feelings.

A sudden smile crossed her face.

"What are you so happy about?" He'd expected anger, hurt or disappointment, but not this.

"I'm singing a duet with DJ Parker. It doesn't get better than that."

He set his guitar in its stand and moved to sit beside Kayla. Her breath caught and she slid to the edge of the other half of the small bench. They sat shoulder to shoulder until he maneuvered to face her a little. "Thank you." He reached for her hand, which rested in her lap. "You're talented. I'm surprised you didn't try and do something with music."

She shrugged. "Honestly, I wanted to have the life you had at one time, but it never happened for me, so I moved on to plan B—college."

A strand of hair rested on her cheek. He thumbed it aside and cradled her cheek in his hand. "I'm glad you chose plan B, or I may never have met you and had this opportunity to sing with you." He kept his voice low, their faces so close her minty breath tickled his chin. He tilted his head. Her lids closed, and their lips met softly.

"What's going on?" Estelle's voice ripped through the quiet room.

Heart pounding, he pulled away from Kayla and released her hand. "What are you doing in here?" he asked, making no effort to hide his annoyance.

"Your mom sent me out to tell you it's time for dinner."

"Ever heard of a cell phone?" He stood and pulled Kayla up with him.

Estelle stood in the doorway with arms crossed and her foot tapping. "Are you coming or not?"

"Please tell my mother I'll be there shortly and to start without me."

"Fine." She pivoted and strutted off.

"Is she always so uptight?" Kayla asked.

"Only when I have friends visiting, which makes no sense considering she's trying to get me to return to LA with her. You'd think she'd pour on the charm *all* the time."

"Maybe she's jealous." Kayla's cheeks turned a pretty shade of light pink.

He waggled his brows. "Does she have something to be jealous about?"

Kayla's forehead crinkled as she pondered Derek's question. Did kissing him really change anything? Clearly they were attracted to one another, and she loved singing with him more than almost anything, but what did it mean? None of that altered the fact he could get bored with their little town and take off. She'd seen that happen so many times with friends she'd grown up with.

One friend in particular stood out in her mind. She

should have known better than to fall for Alex, especially since he matched only half of the qualities on her list. At least he'd never known how she felt about him, or his leaving would have been even more devastating. Last she heard, he lived in Portland, was married and had three kids.

"Kayla?" He stepped toward her, invading her personal space, and held her hands between them. "What do you say? Will you give us another chance?"

"I don't know, Derek. I'm… I just don't know." Her stomach whirled. She loved being with him like this, but was he the one? And more important, was he here to stay? Her heart said yes, but could it be trusted? It'd failed her in the past.

He sighed. "It's fine. I understand." Longing filled his eyes, but he released her hands. "Would you like to stay for dinner? I'm sure there's more than enough."

"No, thanks. I should head home."

"You sure?"

She nodded. His eyes almost begged her to stay, but she needed time to think, and she couldn't do that while sharing a meal with him.

"Okay, then. Is Stan still in town?"

"No. He and my mom flew out this morning for Florida." She liked him so far and hoped his family felt the same way toward her mom. It'd be nice if they could all be one big happy family. "Um, I'm going to go. I'll see you." She turned away before she changed her mind and melted into his arms instead of leaving.

"Meet me here tomorrow after work?"

She looked back and raised a brow. "To work on the float or to sing?"

"Sing. We can finish the float this weekend."

She grinned and nodded before traipsing to her car.

She turned to wave. He stood in the doorway to the barn, his gaze locked on her. Her insides melted from the tender look on his face.

She slid into her car and drove toward home without looking back again. Her cell phone rang. She glanced down. Jill. She'd missed ten calls from her. Her stomach lurched, and she pulled over and put the car in Park. "What's wrong?"

"It's the flower shop." Jill's voice held an edge of panic. "I've been trying to reach you for the past hour!"

"I left my phone in the car. What's wrong with the flower shop?"

"There was a fire on our block and Flowers and More didn't escape it."

"But there's a firewall between all of our businesses. I thought that was supposed to stop fires from spreading."

"I don't know how it happened, but it's not good." Jill's voice said it all.

She leaned her head against the headrest. "How bad?"

"Bad enough we'll have to close the shop for a while. We can work out of my garage, but a friend of mine who's a firefighter said there's a lot of water damage."

"I don't understand how this happened. At least we were closed, and no one was injured. Oh no—was the deli open when the fire happened?"

"Yes. I don't have all the details, but it's pretty ugly down here."

Kayla blinked back unshed tears. "I'll be right there." She pulled back onto the road that led to downtown and pushed the speed limit. Jill sounded so hopeless. Was the situation really that bad? She made a right onto Main Street and gasped. The buildings, illuminated by not only the streetlights but also the kind of lights road crews used at night, looked like a scene out of a war zone.

Windows were shattered, glass covered the sidewalk, and the roofs appeared beyond repair. She wrinkled her nose at the smell. A sick feeling gripped her stomach as she pulled over and parked about a block away from her business. Only one fire truck remained, along with the fire chief's SUV—probably watching any hot spots.

As she walked the block to where Jill stood under the awning of Java World, she prayed that it wasn't as bad as it looked.

Jill's attention turned to her. "It looks bad, huh?"

"Yes. What do you know?"

"I just heard murmurs about an explosion."

"Oh my goodness. Was anyone hurt?"

"Not seriously. Nick at the deli had a good-sized gash on his face, so he's at the hospital getting stitches, but everyone else only has minor cuts and bruises."

Kayla shook her head at the disaster and praised the Lord no one was killed. "Have you been able to get inside our shop to see the damage?"

"Not yet. I was told to wait here."

The sun had gone down over an hour ago and a breeze kicked up, causing Kayla to shiver. "You want coffee?"

"Sure. Thanks."

Kayla stepped into Java World and ordered two large coffees. It looked to be a long night, and they'd need the caffeine. Plus the hot cups would warm their hands. She paid, then headed into the cool evening air. "Here you go. I didn't sweeten it or anything."

"That's fine. I don't care." Cradling the cup between her hands, Jill took a sip. "They make the best coffee. It doesn't even need anything in it to make it taste good."

"True." As if coffee mattered right now. She still couldn't believe the destruction across the street. It was like watching a movie. Only this was real.

The fire chief stepped out of their shop, then crossed the street toward them. Kayla's pulse raced. This was it. Would the shop be a total loss, or was there hope?

Chapter 14

"Oh my! Thanks for calling." Derek's mom hung up the living room phone and turned to him with worry-filled eyes. "There was an explosion downtown. Your friends' shop is damaged."

His heart rate kicked into overdrive. "Kayla left a few minutes ago. When did it happen?"

"About an hour ago."

Estelle walked into the room. "Did you say there was an explosion in town?"

Derek nodded, his heart rate easing. "It sounds bad. I'm going to take a drive and check it out."

"Want company?" Estelle asked. "We should talk."

"Now's not a good time." He couldn't deal with her drama and listen to her try to convince him to return to his singing career. Not when his friends needed him.

"Then when?" She hiked her chin.

"I don't know." He grabbed a jacket from the hook by

the door and jogged to his pickup. Everything had been fine when Kayla had left. How had things gone crazy in such a short time?

Several minutes later he pulled onto Main Street and noticed the block where the flower shop was had been barricaded against traffic. He parked and hustled toward the scene. At least he knew Kayla was okay, since she'd been with him when all this happened. But what about everyone else? He looked both ways and hurried across the street. Kayla and Jill stood shoulder to shoulder talking with the fire chief. He hesitated, unsure if his presence would be welcomed.

Kayla turned her head and did a double take, then motioned him over. "Chief Thompson was filling us in."

"Don't let me interrupt."

The chief nodded. "As I was saying, a small natural-gas explosion took place in the space two doors down from you. The fire is out and the gas is shut off, but we'd like you to wait until morning before entering the building, and then only after it's been inspected to be sure it's structurally sound."

Kayla's eyes widened. Derek grasped her hand and gave it a gentle squeeze. "How is it the buildings are still standing?"

"You mean why didn't the explosion knock out the whole block?" the chief asked.

He nodded.

"It wasn't a huge explosion. The damage is mostly from the fire that quickly spread along the rooftops."

"Which probably destroyed our inventory and our appliances," Jill said.

Derek had never heard Kayla's business partner sound so down. She was always such an upbeat, positive force. It spoke volumes to what Kayla was probably feeling.

"Thank you, Chief," Kayla said.

He nodded and strode across the street.

Jill wrung her hands. "What are we going to do? That store is my life."

Kayla released his hand and pulled her friend into a hug. "We'll figure this out together. At least we have insurance." She stepped back and looked from Jill to him. "For now I suggest we go home and get a good night's sleep because we'll have a full day tomorrow."

Jill nodded. "I suppose I should call Charlie and tell him not to come to work in the morning."

"Why? We'll need his muscle," Kayla said. "Don't worry—everything will be okay."

Jill scowled but didn't argue as she ambled in the opposite direction of where he had parked.

"I'm impressed with how well you are handling this, Kayla. You're stronger than I realized. If you'd like, I could organize a group from the church to help with cleanup."

Kayla's eyes widened and she turned her head to the side. "Thanks for the offer. I'll take all the help we can get. Where are you parked?"

He pointed.

"I'm headed that way, too."

He couldn't stop the grin that spread over his face when she looped her hand through his arm. "This is a nightmare, but I know if the town pulls together, we can have this area cleaned up before the festival in three-and-a-half weeks."

"Oh, man, I forgot about that."

"I didn't. We'll have to work hard and fast, but I'm sure we can pull it off." She stopped beside her car and released his arm. "Thanks for coming down here."

"Sure. When my mom got the call about what happened, all I could think about was your shop. I'm really glad it's not worse."

"Me, too." Although she had seemed confident they'd be able to fix everything and that the town would be ready for the festival, her eyes told another story.

"Hey." He placed a hand on her shoulder. "You know I'm here for you, right? Whatever you need, just ask."

She bit her bottom lip. "I could use a big hug."

His heart melted as he pulled her close. She clung to him. How long they stood like that, he didn't know, but eventually she released her hold and stepped back.

"Thanks. I'll call you tomorrow." She slid into her car, backed out and drove off.

He watched until her taillights disappeared. Now more than ever he knew he belonged in this town pursuing his original dream of leading worship and ministering to the townspeople. A year ago if someone had told him he'd be living in his mother's guest cottage, in a town he'd never laid eyes on, employed as a music pastor and falling head over heels in love with the girl next door, he'd have laughed. Things sure had changed.

He drove back to his mom's place, but rather than head inside, he headed toward the barn and his music studio. Before he got halfway, an all-too-familiar voice stopped him.

"How's your friends' business?" Estelle stepped off the front porch and walked over to him.

"We don't know yet, but it sounds like it may only be water damage on the inside."

"Good. Do you think we could talk now?"

He sighed and ran a hand through his hair. "I suppose, but let's go inside. It's cold tonight."

"Maybe we could chat in the barn. I'd rather talk in private."

He glanced toward the house, then to Estelle. "Is everything okay with my mom?"

"She's fine. She's a tough woman. I don't think her recent fall had any effect on her, other than to annoy her. She still gets a scowl on her face when she brings up that last hospital visit."

"I know. She may never let me live that down. But I had to make sure she wasn't hurt. Maybe I'm being overprotective because of her stroke." He shrugged.

"Talk about things being reversed. The parents are supposed to be the overprotective ones."

"Yeah." He liked this side of Estelle. It reminded him of the good times they'd once shared. He slid the barn door open, then unlocked the door to his studio and flipped on the light. "This is the most comfortable space in the barn."

She looked around and sat on his stool in the center of the room. "It's pretty basic, but it looks like all the necessities are here."

"Thanks. What is it you would like to talk about?" He pulled the chair out from behind the soundboard and sat.

"Your mom has been sharing her faith with me, and I wanted to let you know that I finally understand what's going on with you."

"Oh?"

She chuckled. "Not the answer I expected, but that's okay." She took a deep breath and let it out in a rush of air. "The thing is, I can't go back to LA without you."

"Of course you can. Just get in your car and drive." He softened his words with a half smile.

She shook her head. "You don't understand. Jerry paid me a good deal of money to come here and bring you back. It was my job to talk you into returning to your singing career." She laughed drily. "You must make him a boatload of money."

If this hadn't been Estelle, and if he hadn't been aware of what she was capable of, he'd have laughed at her claim, but it held a note of truth. "Give the money back and be done with him." He made Jerry more money than any of his other clients, so he understood why he'd try to get him to return to singing, but to pay Estelle to get him? It felt off. What was really going on?

"You forget he's *my* manager, too. He's well-known in the industry, and I need him." She looked down and lowered her voice. "The scripts aren't flowing in like they used to."

He blinked. Estelle couldn't land a movie role? She was beautiful and talented. It didn't make sense for an A-list actress like Estelle. Then again, maybe she wasn't on the A-list anymore. It was hard to stay on top with so many willing to do whatever it took to get ahead. Music was his thing, not following who was hot in Hollywood, but now that he thought about it, she'd spent a lot of time volunteering at the children's theater.

He shook his head. "Work may have slowed for you, but trust me, Jerry needs you. His client list has dropped dramatically over the past couple of years. He needs us to fund his lifestyle. Whatever he paid you was a morsel of what he expects to earn in return."

She shook her head. "You don't understand. If I don't do this, he's going to spread lies about me that will keep me unemployed for years, if not forever, in Hollywood."

"That's blackmail. Why would he do that? It wouldn't help him at all if what you say is true." Anger toward his manager boiled. He'd been irritated with Jerry before for telling Estelle where to find him, but now he was downright furious.

She raised a brow. "I already told you, I'm not working. Didn't you think it's strange that I haven't filmed a movie in two years? That flop was the last movie I worked on." She blushed. "I used you to stay in the spotlight, hoping that your success would rub off on my career."

"But then I saw you with Vince." A producer she must

have hoped would find her a spot in an upcoming movie. He shouldn't have been so surprised by her betrayal, but it had hurt.

"Right. And I'm very sorry for using you. I'm sorry for everything, but if Jerry follows through with his threat, I'm finished in Hollywood." She looked at him with glassy eyes. "Maybe I should leave like you did. I'm actually quite the gourmet. I could open my own restaurant."

"I didn't realize you were a cook."

She nodded. "Actually, that's another thing I wanted to talk with you about. I feel horrible about the way I've behaved when your girlfriend is around, and I'd like to make it up to both of you."

"What's the catch?"

"No catch. Your mom's been talking to me a lot about eternity. She actually asked me if God were to say to me today, 'Why should I let you into My heaven?' what would I say?" She shrugged. "I had to tell her He shouldn't. It felt awful to admit that, but your mom led me to Jesus and now I know where I will spend eternity. She told me to pray and to trust God about Jerry, and everything would work out, but I'm scared. This trusting-God business is very hard."

He stilled, only mildly shocked since his mom had said she was sharing the Lord with Estelle. A smile touched his lips and his anger at Jerry simmered down. Estelle was a new Christian! "Trusting Him is an act of faith that can be difficult. But you made a great decision and my mom is right. God will help us with this blackmail situation."

"Us?" She raised a delicate brow.

"That's right. Together we're going to bring him to justice. I know someone in the FBI who may be able to help. Let me give him a call and see what he says. And if you're serious about making things up to me, I have a request." He shared his plan, and she eagerly agreed.

Her shoulders visibly relaxed, and for the first time in a very long time a genuine smile lit her face. "This is going to be fun. Thanks, Derek." She slipped from the room with a bounce in her step.

He rested his head in his hands. What was he going to do? Kayla needed him here, but Jerry couldn't be allowed to get away with this. He pulled his cell from his pocket, looked up his FBI friend's number and called.

Silent tears flowed down Jill's cheeks, and Charlie patted her back with a look of helplessness on his face. Kayla turned from the scene and decided the best way to tackle this mess was one section at a time. Their insurance agent, who had left a few minutes ago, had said it was fine to clean the store.

Their landlord was working on finding a contractor to gut the place, then redo the inside, replace the roof and install a new plate-glass storefront window. Hopefully, all the work would get done quickly so they could reopen as soon as possible. At least the building was determined to be structurally sound, so that would help speed things along.

"Good morning!" Derek walked in carrying a cup tray with four large cups. "I brought coffee." He handed one to each of them, then took the last one for himself.

Kayla sipped hers and her eyes widened. "This is a mocha."

"I thought you would enjoy a treat."

She nodded. "Thanks." She filled him in on everything, then asked about the help he'd promised.

"We were lucky this is a Saturday. The cleaning brigade will be here soon."

"Seriously?" Her voice hitched. "That's wonderful news."

He grinned, then brushed his lips against her forehead. "I promised you help. I always keep my promises."

Kayla's insides tingled, not only from his tender kiss but from his encouraging words. This man was full of surprises.

Derek pushed up his sleeves and got to work tossing soaked, scorched and melted merchandise into large trash bags. Kayla worked alongside Derek, amazed that he would dig into the muck and mire that filled their store.

She stood and stretched like a cat, her attention riveted on the man beside her. His T-shirt strained against the muscles in his back as he hoisted a large black trash bag over his shoulder. He winked as he passed. Her stomach fluttered as if a hundred butterflies occupied it. There was no denying it—the man held a special place in her heart.

Six hours later, sweaty and more tired than she'd ever been, Kayla stood in the middle of Flowers and More and smiled. The space was now ready for construction.

"Thanks to all of you, we did it! Jill and I never could have done this on our own. We're grateful to each of you."

Her friends, some old and some new, cheered and clapped, then slowly filed out the front door.

Derek sidled up beside her. "Pretty soon the place will look brand-new, and you'll have a fresh start."

Kayla turned to face him. "A fresh start. Hmm. I like the sound of that."

"Me, too. How about you and I clean up, then head out for a nice dinner?"

Kayla's pulse picked up. "Yes, I'd like to have dinner with you. Give me an hour?"

"You got it. I'll pick you up at six."

She watched as he stepped out the front door.

"He's perfect," Jill sighed. "You better not mess things up with him. I think he's the one."

Kayla looked over her shoulder at her delirious friend

and laughed. "No one is perfect, but he is pretty cool. As far as being the one? We'll see."

Charlie pushed through the swinging door from the back room. "The roofers are taking off. I have to hand it to your landlord, not only did he secure a crew in short order, but there are so many of them the job will be finished in no time."

Kayla shouldered her purse. "Yeah, he's pretty impressive. Being back in business before the festival is looking more like a possibility. Will the two of you lock up? I have a hot date."

Jill waved her away. "We've got this. Have fun."

Kayla rushed from the shop. She didn't have much time to shower and get ready for her date, and she wanted to look her best.

Forty-five minutes later her doorbell pealed. She charged down the stairs, not wanting to keep Derek waiting. She'd chosen a long white skirt with a red blouse and red ballet flats. The ensemble made her feel pretty, which was exactly what she'd been going for.

She pulled open the door and grinned. "Hi."

"Hi, yourself." Derek's eyes held appreciation. "You ready?"

"Just let me lock up." Her stomach growled. "Where are we eating?"

"It's a surprise."

"Oh no. The last time someone said that to me, I found out I was getting a stepdad. May I at least have a hint?"

He chuckled, took her hand and tucked it around his arm. "Nope." A silly grin covered his face as he pulled his pickup door open and helped her inside.

What did Derek have planned? She hopped inside and clasped her hands, willing her pulse to slow.

Chapter 15

Kayla's eyes widened as Derek pulled into his mother's driveway. "We're eating dinner at your mom's house?" Hadn't he suggested a nice restaurant?

"Not exactly. Have patience. I don't want to slip up and spoil the surprise."

Kayla nodded and tried to keep an open mind. Not that she minded Helen or even Estelle at this point, but she'd hoped for a romantic meal alone with Derek. He parked near the barn. She jumped out. "Are we eating in the barn?"

"Shh." He touched a gentle finger to her lips, then guided her along a path that meandered between the house and barn. They looped around toward the back of the house and stopped on a footbridge.

Twinkle lights lit the backyard, and a darling cottage stood at the edge. Kayla caught her breath. "This is beautiful. I had no idea this was back here."

"No? Remember me telling you I was staying in the guest cottage?"

"Now that you mention it, I guess I do." She grinned. "But I had no idea what a paradise your mother's backyard is."

He wrapped his arms around her and pulled her close. "I'm glad you're here." He kissed her lightly, then stepped back and took her hand. "Come on. Dinner is waiting."

He pushed the door open with a flourish. "Welcome to Casa Derek. After you."

Kayla stepped inside the quaint home. It was essentially a studio, with a curtained-off sleeping area, a small dining table, a kitchenette, a cozy living room and a door she presumed led to the bathroom. The table was set with silver-trimmed white plates, simple goblets and two red taper candles. "It's beautiful." She breathed in deeply. "Rosemary?"

He nodded and guided her to the table.

"How did you have time to pull this off?"

"A friend helped, and the food is catered."

"You found a caterer on such short notice?"

He shook his head. "I actually set this up last night with the hope you'd say yes."

She raised her eyebrows. "What if I'd said no?"

"Then I would have had the most amazing prime rib, roasted vegetables, homemade rolls and apple pie à la mode to myself." He gently guided her to the table and pulled out her chair.

"I'm glad I said yes." She sat and looked up at him.

His eyes danced. "Me, too."

He stepped into the kitchenette, opened the small oven, then pulled out a platter.

"Oh my goodness. It's beautiful. Who cooked this? I had no idea Oak Knoll had a caterer."

"A friend. She's technically not a caterer, just passionate about cooking." He placed the platter on the table, then offered a blessing for the food.

After serving herself, Kayla took a bite of the melt-in-your-mouth meat. "Whoever your friend is, she could make a killing if she did this full-time."

"I'll let her know you said so. She mentioned she's considering opening a restaurant."

"With food like this, she'd be a hit." Kayla tasted the vegetables and almost sighed with contentment but caught herself. "Wow. Please give your friend my compliments."

Derek grinned. "Will do." He forked a bite of beef into his mouth and chewed.

Kayla looked around the cottage admiring the little touches. Lace curtains covered the windows and a simple white couch faced a natural-gas fireplace—not exactly a bachelor pad, but it had touches of homeyness that made her want to stay awhile. She liked her own house, but this place was the next best thing. "Your mom has done an incredible job."

He looked around the room. "It's cozy." He placed his napkin aside. "Dessert?"

"Not yet. I need to digest."

He pushed back from the table and moved to the wall beside the fireplace. "I'll light the fire and we can visit on the couch."

"I'd like that." She stood and walked the few steps to the couch as he flicked the switch on the wall. "That's definitely easier than lighting a fire the old-fashioned way." She settled into one corner of the couch.

"For sure." He dropped into the other corner and sat facing her. "I'm really glad you came tonight because there's something I need to tell you, and I want you to hear it from me."

Kayla's throat tightened. From the look on his face, this had to be bad news. She took a deep breath and let it out slowly. "Okay."

"I'm leaving for Los Angeles on Sunday, after church."

Kayla gasped. The dinner she'd just devoured turned sour. She fought to control her emotions. *He's leaving.* "I see. Thank you for telling me." *Especially before I made a fool out of myself and declared my undying love!*

"I should only be gone a week at the most."

The tension flowing through her eased. Too bad he hadn't opened with he'd be gone only a week. She'd about lost her meal at the thought of him walking out of her life for good.

"You wouldn't believe what my manager is trying to pull. I actually had to call the FBI for help. It's the kind of thing you'd see in the movies."

"Huh?" She shook her head, as if the motion would clear up everything. "What are you talking about?"

"Estelle is being blackmailed by our manager. As it turns out, the FBI was already investigating him. They want Estelle to return to Los Angeles and give a statement."

"Oh, wow." Her stomach tensed. "Why are *you* going? Is he blackmailing you, too?"

"No. But it's because of me he's doing this. Jerry is a desperate man, and he's angry because I left. I've made him millions."

For the first time Kayla had a hint of exactly how wealthy Derek was and what he was giving up. He acted like such a regular guy. But she didn't care that he was rich. She was proud of him for doing the right thing but was concerned about the timing. "What if you aren't back in time for the festival?"

He scooted closer to her on the couch and reached for her hand. "I promise no matter what happens, I will be here." His eyes spoke sincerity, but sincerity didn't change the legal system should he be required to stay longer than he anticipated.

The growing knot in her stomach tightened. "What about our duet?"

"We already sound great, so there's nothing to worry about. Any practice we get is a bonus."

"What about your worship position at the church?"

He frowned. "I hope to be back by Sunday, but Pastor Miller knows what's going on."

"Okay." It seemed as though he had thought of everything. She would miss him, but he was doing the right thing. A lone tear escaped and she quickly swiped it away.

"Hey," he said softly, and tipped her chin up with a finger. "You're taking this way too hard. What's up?"

She shrugged. "It's nothing." She offered him a quivery smile. "I'll miss you. You've turned into my knight in shining armor."

"Ah, Kayla, you're killing me." He pulled her close.

She nestled into his embrace and relished the comfort of his arms. A few tears slipped out and were soaked up by his soft shirt. She pushed back. "I don't know why I'm being such a baby. I'm sorry. It's not fair to you that I behave like this. I get emotional when I'm overly tired. I didn't sleep well last night and cleaning the shop today wore me out."

Derek's heart melted at Kayla's words. He pulled her close and wrapped his arms around her. "It's okay." Now that Kayla had pointed out how tired she was, her tears made sense. His mom did the same thing when she was wiped out. Maybe asking Kayla to dinner after all she'd been through in the past twenty-four hours had been selfish, but he didn't want to leave town without telling her what was going on. He placed a kiss on the top of her head.

With a shuddering breath, she pulled from his embrace. "Thanks for the meal and for everything you did today."

"You're welcome."

Three quick taps sounded on the door. Who could that be? "Excuse me." He marched the short distance to the door and swung it open. "Estelle. What are you doing here?"

"I came for the dishes. Your mom went to bed early, and I'm bored."

"Oh." He stepped aside, allowing her to enter. His gaze landed on Kayla's shocked face. "Estelle was our caterer. She's here for cleanup."

Kayla hopped up. "You cook, Estelle? I had no idea." The pitch of her voice rose. She moved around the couch and into the dining area, where she helped Estelle clear the table. Weariness covered her face and her movements were slower than normal, but he had to give her credit for helping out in spite of being worn out.

"I read that you have a private chef who cooks for you."

"I did for a short while, and she was amazing. I was so fascinated by her culinary creations I convinced her to teach me some dishes so I could impress my guests from time to time." She grinned. "Cooking is therapeutic, and I've missed it since I've been here. But that will all change soon."

"Yeah, I heard about your manager."

Estelle's brow furrowed. "I hope you keep that to yourself." She shot an annoyed look at Derek.

"What? I had to tell her. I couldn't leave town without an explanation."

"Didn't stop you before," she snapped. Her shoulders drooped. "Sorry. That wasn't nice." She offered an apologetic smile to Kayla. "I'm working on being kind even when I'm stressed. Which I am."

"Because of the statement you're going to give the FBI?"

She nodded. "If the press gets hold of this…ugh. I don't even want to go there."

Derek pitched in and soon the dishes and leftovers were neatly stacked in the box he'd used to carry everything over. "I'll be right back, Kayla."

Estelle reached for the door, then stopped and turned to Kayla. "I'm sorry for being such a difficult person. I went out of my way to be unpleasant to you, and I hope you'll forgive me."

"Of course." Kayla's eyes widened. "I hope everything works out for you."

"Thanks." She stepped into the backyard and tromped ahead of Derek.

"You okay, Estelle?" Derek asked as he followed her inside his mom's house.

"Just nervous, but I'll be fine."

"There's a Bible on the bookshelf in the study. Maybe you'll find comfort in reading it. My favorite verse is Jeremiah 29:11. It says, 'For I know the plans I have for you, declares the Lord, plans to prosper you and not to harm you, plans to give you hope and a future.'"

"What does that mean?" In the kitchen she pushed the faucet to hot, then squirted soap into the sink.

"It means God loves you so much that He has a plan for your life and He's going to take care of you. So don't worry. He's got everything under control even when things seem out of control."

A smile stretched her lips. "Thanks." She nudged his shoulder. "Now go back to your woman."

He grinned. "Good night, Estelle. See you at church?"

She scrunched her nose. "Do you think that's a good idea? I heard you talking with your friends about your fans in the service, and I don't want to create a scene."

"They promised the pastor that they'd be on their best behavior from now on. Come or don't. Either way, we'll head out right after service." He hustled to the door and across the yard to the cottage, where he found Kayla asleep on the couch, her head tipped to the side, and her lips parted slightly. He knelt in front of her. "Hey, sleepyhead."

Her eyelids fluttered open. "I guess I'm even more tired than I realized."

He chuckled. "I'll take you home." He stood and held out a hand. "Let's go." They walked hand in hand to his pickup. Crickets chirped, filling the otherwise quiet night air. Pulling the door open, he waited for Kayla to slip in. Then he jogged to the driver's side and hopped in. "Do you mind if I ask you a personal question?"

"I'm not sure. What's the question?"

"I heard that you have a *list*, and that you were once Miss Teen Oregon." He put the truck in gear and pulled out.

She gasped. "How?"

"The church janitor."

She crossed her arms and stared straight ahead. "Figures."

He would have laughed but feared she might bite his head off. "I take it you're not happy he told me."

"More like I'm mortified. For the record, that pageant was *not* my idea. When I was sixteen, I won the title of runner-up in the Miss Oregon Teen pageant. I'm proud about what I accomplished, but you have no clue what I went through because of that thing."

"Then maybe you should tell me."

She buried her head in her hands for a second and groaned before pulling them away. "This is embarrassing. However, it happened a long time ago, so I'll try to muddle through it. When I took runner-up in the pageant, I became Miss Popular at school. The guys… Well, I had no shortage of dates. The problem was none of those guys cared about me. They only wanted to go out with me because of the pageant.

"At first all the attention went to my head. I was even dumb enough to fall for one of the guys. It turned out he was only with me to stroke his ego. He didn't care about me, other than what I did for his social status."

Her story sounded so much like his own. "What happened?" He almost didn't want to know, but his insides burned with anger for the way this punk had treated her.

"I can't… Let's just say he was the reason I created 'the list.'" She made air quotes with her fingers.

Now things were beginning to make sense. "Are you still using the list?"

"Kind of." Her voice came out weak.

"How do I rank?"

"Higher than anyone ever has."

He grinned and sat a little taller.

"But…"

Oh no. He did *not* like that word. He braced himself for whatever she was about to say.

"It's not important. You're leaving tomorrow and, well, I don't see how it matters."

"I'll be back. It matters."

"We'll see. I know you believe what you're saying, but the lure of fame and fortune is a lot to give up. Once you're back there, you may change your mind."

He gripped the steering wheel tighter. "Then I guess you'll have to trust me, won't you?"

Chapter 16

Derek sat at a conference table in a too-small room of the Los Angeles FBI field office. Unease wrapped its tentacles around him. FBI Special Agent Price stood at the head of the table in a black suit and nondescript tie. Everything about the agent was nondescript except his personality, which was sorely lacking compassion.

"Mr. Wood, I understand why you don't want to go along with this plan, but it is the only way to protect Miss Rogers." The agent shot an admiring glance toward Estelle.

This was *not* what he wanted. He ran a hand through his hair, wishing he were back in Oak Knoll, where men like Special Agent Price didn't exist. Apparently he was expected to return to business as usual in order to convince Jerry he'd won so he wouldn't destroy Estelle's career. "When I came here, it was as moral support, not to get involved in some FBI operation. Why can't you arrest Jerry? You have him on blackmail charges. Isn't that enough?"

"Sir. There is more at stake here than blackmail, but I'm not at liberty to say anything further. You may choose not to do this, but Miss Rogers will pay the price with her reputation if you don't help. We all know Mr. Smith will follow through with his threat."

He ground his teeth and stifled a growl of frustration. "Fine, but I need to be back in Oak Knoll by April twenty-ninth."

"We will do our best to have this wrapped up by then. Do you understand what we need you to do?"

"Yes. I go to the recording studio tomorrow and begin work on my next album, which, for the record, is a complete waste of time and money." He had no intention of finishing the album.

"There are things in play you don't know about. If you are at the studio, we can keep you safe. Understand?"

Derek nodded, suddenly feeling like a spoiled child. He could only assume the FBI had imbedded agents into the studio for their investigation and would be there if anything went wrong. But what did the studio have to do with Jerry? He'd never worked with this studio. "If we're done here…?"

"Yes. We'll be in touch. Remember, act normal."

"Right." Normal? What was normal anymore? Was normal living the high life here in LA, or was it spending his days working on church and community business? He knew which one he *wanted* to be normal and it included plenty of time with Kayla. He glanced at Estelle. "You ready to get out of here?"

She nodded and stood. "Thank you for doing this. I know it's a sacrifice, and if there was any other way—"

"It's not your fault Jerry is a lying, thieving, lawbreaking scumbag."

Estelle chuckled. "Sorry, but I've never heard you talk like that."

He shrugged. "First time for everything. Right?" What was he going to tell his mom? She expected him to take the red-eye and be home by morning.

After dropping Estelle at her house, he headed to a hotel since he'd sublet his condo when he'd left for Italy.

Lord, please help this to be over with quickly.

He pulled his cell from his pocket and called his mom. She answered on the first ring. "Hey, Mom. I wanted you to know I'm here, and it looks like I'm going to be away longer than I thought." He explained the situation. "If you need anything—"

"I have friends, so stop worrying." Her words, though still a little slow, were clear, and that put a smile on his face. She had made remarkable progress.

"Okay. Love you."

"Love you, too. Be careful."

"I will. Bye." He punched in Kayla's number and waited and waited. Voice mail picked up. "Kayla, it's Derek. Things here are going to take longer than I thought. I'm really sorry. I'll try to catch you later." He disconnected the call. Now what?

In the old days he'd go out to a nice restaurant, then hit a club to keep his face in the tabloids. Clubbing wasn't his thing and he'd stayed only long enough for the paparazzi to snap his picture.

Jerry would expect him to fall into his old patterns and might become suspicious if he stayed in. But it was his first night back, and he was due in the studio early tomorrow. Jerry must have had this booked for months anticipating he'd be back. He'd just grab a bite in the hotel restaurant after he checked in.

He pulled into the Hilton and parked. His cell phone played the tune he'd assigned to Kayla. "Hey there."

"Hey, yourself. I got your message. Is everything okay?"

"Not exactly, but it will be soon, I hope."

"Cryptic."

"Sorry." He told her what was going on. "I wish I could say I'll be home soon like I'd planned, but things here aren't what I expected."

"It's okay. You're doing the right thing and that's what's important."

"Thanks for understanding. How is everything there?"

"A construction crew gutted the shop today. I'm still hoping everything will be finished by the festival, but it will be close."

He already missed seeing her sparkling eyes. "While I'm gone, we should plan to talk on Skype."

"That's a great idea!"

Derek's lips stretched into a smile. Maybe being here wouldn't be so miserable after all. At least he had something to look forward to.

From her window seat at Java World, Kayla watched as two men replaced the front window of Flowers and More. In a week and a half the construction crew had made incredible progress. Best of all, their landlord said it'd be finished by this weekend, which meant with a lot of hard work their grand reopening would coincide with the festival.

She sipped her coffee and made a mental list of all that needed to be done. Jill had taken the vacation she'd encouraged Kayla to take and would be back on Friday—perfect timing. She probably should have taken the chance to get away, too, but there were so many festival details to tend to that taking off would not have been relaxing.

"Hey there. I thought I might find you here."

Kayla looked to her left. "Mom." She jumped up and hugged her. "When did you get home?"

"Just drove into town and saw your car." Her mom pulled out a chair and sat.

Kayla reached for her purse. "Would you like a coffee?"

"I ordered a latte."

The barista called out her mother's name and she stood. "Be right back." A moment later Mom sat and cradled a mug. "How are you doing?"

"I've been better, but all things considered, things are moving along well."

Mom nodded. "What about Derek? Any word when he'll be back?"

"No." Sadness washed through Kayla at the mention of his name. She'd been trying to avoid thinking about him, instead keeping her focus on the festival, because the longer he was gone, the more she missed him and then her imagination took flight.

Mom reached across the table and rested her hand on Kayla's. "What is it, sweetie?"

Kayla started. Her mom was too perceptive. "I thought I was doing a good job hiding my unease."

She chuckled. "I'm your mother. You can't fool me. What's wrong?"

"Besides the fact my store was destroyed, the festival starts next week and..." *The man I love isn't here.*

"And?"

Kayla shook her head. "It's silly, but I miss Derek."

"There's nothing silly about that."

"Thanks. You never said when the big day is." While Mom was in Florida meeting with Stan's family, she'd talked with her quite a lot. His kids were understandably shocked by their announcement, but they'd eventually warmed up to her.

"We were thinking we might elope. We've both been married before, and neither of us wants to plan a big wedding."

"Hmm. Okay. What about a reception? You could do a small one here and one in Florida for his friends and family."

"That's a lovely idea. I'll see what Stan thinks." Mom cleared her throat. "I hate to bring this up now, but I know how you need time to chew on things."

Kayla's shoulders tensed.

"I'm moving to Florida once we're married."

The tension in her shoulders eased. "Oh, is that all? I thought… Actually, I don't know what I thought. But I expected you to move there. With his law practice, he couldn't pick up and move here."

She beamed a smile. "Thank you for understanding. I was afraid you'd be upset."

"I'll miss you, but now I know where to go for that vacation I've been talking about taking."

"Wonderful!" Mom got to her feet, holding the latte she hadn't even taken a sip of. "I have laundry to do, and I want to call Stan. I'll see you later." She breezed outside and disappeared from sight.

Kayla resumed her vigil of watching over the store's progress. The new plate-glass window seemed bare without the store's name painted on it, but Jill would take care of that this weekend.

Her cell jingled a new tune she'd just bought—a DJ Parker song she'd assigned to his number. "Hi, Derek."

"Hi, yourself. How's it going?"

"Things at the store are moving along well, and I was told we can move in this coming weekend."

"That's great. I wish I could be there to help."

She tried very hard not to be disappointed. "No worries. Charlie will be there, and I think he was able to get a small army to help with the heavy stuff."

"Good."

"You're still planning to be here for the festival, right?"

"Of course."

She heard voices rumble through the phone. "It sounds like you're busy."

"Yeah. We're recording today."

"Are you really going to put out a new album?"

"It looks that way. I still can't believe how quickly this thing came together. It helped that I'd already written half the songs."

Kayla swallowed the lump in her throat. "Yeah, I imagine that helped a lot." The longer he was gone, the more it felt as if he was never coming back. She knew how things worked. If he released a new album, there would be a publicity tour, concerts, television appearances…

"I need to go. Don't forget our Skype session next week."

"I won't. Bye." She laid the phone on the table and sighed. She had to keep reminding herself why he was doing what he was doing—it was the right thing. People were counting on him, and she could get along without him. But when would he return?

Chapter 17

Derek stared out the window of the FBI conference room. He never liked Mondays and today was no exception. He worked his jaw in an effort to keep his temper under control. After taking a few deeps breaths to calm down, he turned to face Special Agent Price. "I'm supposed to be in Oregon on Friday morning. I'm pulling a parade float that I built, and on the last night of the festival, I'm doing a concert. I need this to *end*."

"I hear you. And I need you to trust me and continue to do what you are doing."

"Jerry is on my case about living in a hotel. What do you suggest I tell him?" He crossed his arms.

"That you sublet your condo."

"I did. He told me to kick the guy out."

Price's jaw tightened, and he looked ready to lose his temper. Maybe Derek had sounded petty and pushed too hard to end this, but they were entering the week of the festival, and he'd never expected to still be in Los Angeles. He'd made a promise to Kayla, and he wanted to keep it. But there was no way he'd leave until Jerry was behind bars, or it all would have been for nothing. Jerry expected the old Derek. The performer who followed his instructions and put his career above all else.

"I don't care what you tell him—just make it believable. What does Jerry have planned for you this coming weekend?"

The glint in Agent Price's eyes made his stomach knot. The man's normal coolness was replaced by an edge Derek was unaccustomed to seeing. Was something going to happen soon? "He said something about a nightclub on Saturday night, but I don't know. I *need* to be in *Oregon*."

"I know. We are very close to making an arrest, and I don't want you doing anything that will spook him. Go along with whatever he wants. I'll be in touch." He opened the door and motioned for Derek to leave. "And, Derek?"

He turned back with a raised brow.

"You're doing a great job. You know I can't give any details, but everything is going to work out. And one more thing. No more contact with your girlfriend or anyone else back home until this over."

"Why? Did I do something to tip Jerry off?"

He shook his head. "The man is getting nervous. Something big is coming up and he's jumpy. That's more than I should have said. Don't worry—you're safe. We just don't want an overheard or intercepted conversation to compromise all that we've been doing."

A surge of anger gripped him. It was a good thing the FBI was involved, because Jerry had stepped over the line. He didn't bother questioning Price further. Kayla would understand once he was home and able to explain. At least this craziness was almost over. The thought eased his anger and with a little extra spring in his step, he headed to the studio to meet with the record label. An hour later he pulled into the lot and walked in through the double glass doors.

"Good afternoon, Mr. Parker," a young receptionist greeted him.

He lifted his chin and raised a hand.

"Mr. Holder said to meet him in his office. Sixth floor."

Derek almost stopped but forced his feet to move. Why would the president of the company want to meet with him? Sure, he was a big name for the label, but Holder had never requested a meeting before. He pressed the up arrow and stepped onto the elevator. The doors slid closed and he was whisked up to the sixth floor without a single stop.

He stepped out and spotted another young receptionist. She raised a finger to him without even looking up. He stood quietly and waited. She flipped a magazine page, then looked at him. Her eyes widened. "Oh, I'm sorry. I didn't know it was you. Mr. Holder is waiting for you." She bounded up. "Follow me, please. You should have told me it was you."

"I thought you might be on the phone or doing something important, but I guess reading *Rolling Stone* magazine is important around here."

Her face reddened. At least she had the grace to look embarrassed. He didn't mind her rudeness. It had given him a couple of minutes to calm himself.

She knocked and entered. "Mr. Holder, Mr. Parker is here to see you."

"Thank you, Lila. Please close the door on your way out." Mr. Holder rose and offered a fist. "Thanks for coming."

Derek bumped the man's knuckles. "Of course."

"Have a seat." The plump man in somewhat conservative attire motioned to the plush leather chair facing the desk. He sat behind his desk and steepled his fingers in front of his face, resting his pointer finger on his crooked nose. "I've been hearing a lot about this new album you've been working on. In fact, I listened to the album."

"And?"

"It's your best ever. The songs are fresh with a new vibe. I want to go big with this. The top publicist in the area is on call, ready to create so much buzz this album will rocket to number one the day it releases. I want to do a six-month tour beginning in New York, and I'm calling in a favor to get you on *Dick Clark's New Year's Rockin' Eve* special." He slid a packet of papers across the desk. "It's your time. You are going to be bigger than ever, DJ. Every household in America will know the name DJ Parker. All you need to do is sign."

Derek's heart hammered. Something wasn't right. "I'll pass this on to my manager. Let him take a look."

Holder narrowed his eyes. "About Jerry—the man is on his way out. Everyone but you seems to know it. Cut him loose."

Derek forced a cocky grin. "Yeah, I've heard rumors, but you know how it is—he was there for me in the beginning. I'll get back to you."

"Loyalty to deadweight won't get you very far, DJ. Don't wait too long. That offer expires in forty-eight hours."

Derek stood and snagged the contract. "I'll get back to you. Thanks." He had only one question, and Special Agent Price had better have a good answer. Who had paid for this album to be produced? He'd assumed the label had worked out a deal with Jerry, but it now appeared otherwise. Could the FBI have pulled this off?

He passed by the receptionist's desk. She quickly ended a call when she spotted him. She stood, all smiles, with her hands clutched behind her back. "That was fast."

"Yep. See you." He sauntered toward the elevator. What was he supposed to do with the contract? One thing was certain: Jerry could never see it.

His cell buzzed in his pocket. He checked the caller ID—Kayla. His shoulders slumped, and he stuffed the phone away. This wasn't fair to her, but she knew what he was doing. If only he could have warned her about not being able to communicate. He looked around to see if anyone was watching him and spotted a camera mounted near the ceiling. If Price was right, everything he said could be being recorded, and he didn't want to jeopardize the operation.

The elevator doors slid open, and he stepped in. He rode it to the lobby. Maybe he could get Price to call Kayla? When the doors slid open, a camera flashed, and a microphone was pushed in his face.

"When will your album release, DJ?"

"No comment." He pushed past the reporter.

"Why so secretive?"

He kept walking without looking back. Clearly that had been a setup, and he suspected he knew by whom. Once in his rental car, he speed-dialed the secure number for Special Agent Price with a burner phone he'd been given in case of an emergency. "I have a situation." He explained what had gone down.

"You did great. Continue to evade their questions. Sign the contract or not. I don't care, but since it was imperative to this operation, your studio time was paid for by the bureau. You are under no obligation to sign a contract with the label."

For the first time since he'd been told Holder wanted to see him, he breathed easy. "Thanks."

"Don't call again, Derek. I'll be in touch."

"What do you mean? I'm not allowed to contact the FBI again?"

"Exactly. This number is for emergency purposes only."

The background noise from Price's end silenced. The man had hung up! And he hadn't even had a chance to ask him to contact Kayla. He flicked the phone onto the passenger seat. "I can't wait for this to end." He shoved the car into gear and peeled out. *Sign the contract or not* played over and over in his mind as he drove. He didn't want to sign. Did he? It was the opportunity of a lifetime, and he'd be nuts to turn it down. But he'd left all of that behind. A part of him was exhilarated by the offer, but his stomach was in a knot. And what about Mom and Kayla?

No question, he had a lot to consider. He'd happened to notice the terms of the contract, and it was generous. It would take only six months or maybe even less to promote the album, and then he'd be free to walk—and his finances would be set for life and then some, especially if he continued to live in Oak Knoll.

Kayla sat on her living room couch with a bowl of popcorn and the remote control watching the evening news. A commercial came on for a gossip program, and a picture of Derek flashed across the screen. She leaned forward and raised the volume.

"DJ Parker is rumored to have signed with Holly Records."

Kayla switched off the TV and stared at the black screen. What were they talking about? This had to be part of the FBI sting. But what if Derek changed his mind and the deal they offered was too sweet to pass on? The last time they'd spoken, he'd mentioned that he wanted to start a new chapter in his life. She'd assumed he was talking about finishing up his obligation to the FBI and then coming home. But what if he meant signing with a new record label?

No, she didn't believe it. The FBI must have arranged the news so Jerry would play into their hand. But just to be certain, she'd ask Derek. He hadn't picked up earlier when she'd called to ask about the parade float, but hopefully, he'd pick up this time. She grabbed her cell phone and called. After seven rings his voice mail kicked on. "Hi, Derek, it's me, Kayla. I need to talk with you about the float, and I saw a teaser on TV tonight saying you'd signed with a new label. What's that all about? Well…I guess that's all. Please call me. Bye."

She set the phone on the cushion beside her, doing her best to stay calm and rational. But she wasn't very good at either when her heart was involved. She hopped up, wishing for a hobby like jogging or bicycling—something that would help her calm down. The keyboard in the corner of the room drew her. She might not be ultraphysical, but playing the keyboard had always been able to soothe her.

The front door slammed. "Oops. Sorry!" Mom strolled into the room. "It's windy this evening."

Kayla nodded and moved to her keyboard. "Will it bother you if I play for a while?"

"Not at all. I enjoy hearing you play. It's been a while."

Kayla powered on the instrument and sat. She started with a few scales to get her fingers moving, then jumped into Schumann's "The Wild Horseman." The energy in the song mirrored her mood. Next, Bach's "Solfeggietto" flowed off her fingers, her emotions once again matching the music. After several more aggressive pieces, she calmed and moved into worship songs. Peace finally washed through her. She closed her eyes and started singing "The Heart of Worship" by Matt Redman. At the end of the song she slowly lifted her hands from the keys and opened her eyes.

"I haven't heard you play and sing like that in a long time."

Mom's quiet voice startled her. Caught up in the music, she'd forgotten she was there. "It's been a while since I *needed* to."

Her mom nodded. "I hope I wasn't the cause of whatever is bothering you. If my getting married upsets you—"

"No." Kayla stood and hurried to the couch where her mom sat. "I'm very happy for you and relieved that Stan's kids accepted you. Their attitude was my only hesitation, and clearly my fears were unfounded." She didn't want to talk about Derek. Some things were best left unsaid. "When you set a date, let me know. I'd like to be there."

"Really? We were planning to marry in Vegas."

Kayla's mouth opened, and she snapped it shut. "For real?"

"Yep. Since I may never get to Paris, I asked Stan if we could stay at the Paris Las Vegas Hotel after we're married. He loved the idea."

"I don't want to crash your honeymoon. I'll wait for your reception."

"You are more than welcome to come to our wedding. It will be fun. I think Stan's kids may be there. It'd be a good opportunity to meet them."

Kayla hesitated for only a moment. If her mom wanted her there, she wouldn't say no. "Okay, count me in."

Mom's face split into a smile that reached her sparkling eyes. "Thanks. I feel like a young bride. I'm so excited."

"What will you wear?"

"I have a style in mind. Maybe you and I could go shopping together."

"I'd like that. But *after* the festival."

"You got it." Mom stood and left the room.

Kayla checked her phone in case Derek had called and

she'd missed it—nothing. Unease threatened to hold her in its clutches once more, but she refused to succumb.

Mom poked her head around the corner. "By the way, who is riding on your float?"

"Oh no! I completely forgot about finding someone after all the drawing entries we had at the shop were destroyed. I don't know what to do."

Mom pressed her lips together. "What about talking to the high school? Maybe they can run a little competition and the winner gets to ride on the float."

"That could work. I'll call the school first thing tomorrow. Thanks!"

"That's what I'm here for. Is the float finished?"

"All except for some fresh flowers and plants that Jill and I will add the night before."

"Wonderful. And here you thought it couldn't be done. Look at all you've accomplished."

"Well, if I'd been working in the store for the past two weeks, it wouldn't have been done, but since I've been able to focus on festival stuff, it wasn't too big of a project."

Mom grinned. "Isn't it nice how everything has worked out?" She slipped around the corner.

How her mom managed to find the good in all situations escaped her, but she was right. The timing had actually worked to her advantage and thanks to her exceptional landlord, the flower shop would open in time for the festival. Yes, everything was falling into place perfectly. Well, almost everything. There still was the matter of Derek. What if he wasn't back in time? What would they do? There was no backup plan for the concert. *He* was the backup plan.

Chapter 18

Kayla knocked on Helen's door, her heart hammering in her chest. Derek not only missed their Skype session this week, but he wasn't answering any of her calls.

Derek's mom pulled the door open. A smile lit her eyes, and she motioned for Kayla to come in.

She followed Helen into the kitchen, where she pulled out a chair. "Sit. I was getting ready to have tea. Would you like some?" Kayla nodded and sat in the chair. She stilled her fidgeting fingers by folding them in her lap.

Helen poured hot water into two cups and placed a basket filled with tea bags on the table.

"Thank you, Helen." She hadn't planned to stay but didn't have the heart to leave her alone when she so clearly wanted company. "Have you heard from Derek this week?"

She shook her head as she sat.

"It's being reported on TV that he signed a music deal with Holly Records. Did he say anything to you about it?"

She cradled a teacup in her hands. "Derek will do the right thing. I trust my boy and you should, too."

"I do trust him, but I'm confused. Everything was going so well, and now he won't even return my calls."

Helen smiled. "Kayla, I like you. You're a nice young woman and I like that my son cares for you."

Kayla bit her bottom lip to keep from interrupting as Helen struggled to spit out the rest of what was on her mind.

"I learned a long time ago to stop worrying about Derek and put my trust in the Lord. You should, too.

"He's in control and no matter how much you worry, it won't change anything."

"You're right, but I'm concerned. The parade is tomorrow morning, and he promised he'd be here, but he's not."

Helen nodded. "Charlie stopped by earlier. He'll drive Derek's truck and pull the float."

Well, at least the float was covered. "I guess I should have checked with Jill or Charlie before bothering you. I'm sorry."

"Don't be. I enjoy the company."

"Jill will be here soon with the flowers and foliage for the finishing touches on the float. Feel free to come out to the barn and keep us company."

Helen grinned. "Thanks, but I think I'll stay inside."

"Okay. I should head out now. If Derek calls, will you ask him to touch base with me?"

She nodded.

Kayla stood and took her half-empty teacup to the sink. Helen led her to the front door and pulled it open. "Come visit anytime."

"Thanks, Helen." She spun around and marched to the barn. The shop's delivery van was parked right outside the barn door and Jill stood beside it. "Hey there, I didn't hear you drive up. Have you been here long?"

"Five minutes tops." Jill held a bucket filled with hot-pink carnations that popped against her newly tanned skin. Her friend had spent every day of her vacation lounging on the beach. Relaxing sounded wonderful. Only three more days and then life would go back to normal.

"Are you excited about the grand opening tomorrow?" Jill asked as she led the way into the barn where the float was stored.

"Yes, but I have so much going on—it's stressful. At least all the volunteers I'm in charge of confirmed they will be at their shifts tomorrow."

"There's something to be thankful for." Jill hopped onto the float and went directly to the arbor. "I thought we could create a trellis of carnations, but now that I'm here, I don't like the idea."

"I'd say don't bother with any flowers, but since we are a florist, we should make sure there are plenty. Skip the arbor. I'm thinking Rose Parade–type float."

Jill laughed. "Not happening."

"Why?" It wasn't like Jill to not even consider a good idea.

"Do you have any idea how many man-hours it would take to pull that off? Not to mention all the flowers. No way, no how is this going to pass for a Rose Parade float, but it will look fantastic."

Kayla watched her friend work and jumped in once she figured out what Jill was doing. They created a flower garden all around the arbor where the winner from the contest the high school held would be seated. Jill was right—this was going to look great. It might even win an award.

Kayla hopped off the float. "What we did looks fabulous, but now the rest looks bare."

"Have faith, my friend. We are only getting started. I hope you are rested up, because this may take most of the night."

"Shut up. Please tell me you are joking."

"I'm exaggerating a little, but I was serious. Don't worry. My mom is coming over and bringing several of her friends to help. Actually, considering all the helping hands she's bringing, we might be out of here in under an hour, now that I see what we accomplished in such a short time. Will you grab the vines from the van?"

"Sure." On her way back inside, she overheard Jill on the phone talking to someone about Derek. Curious, she couldn't help listening in. When Jill spotted her, she ended the call. "What was that about?"

Jill frowned. "I was hoping to spare you from Margie, but she is having a conniption because Derek hasn't been seen in nearly three weeks. She's afraid he's going to be a no-show for the concert Sunday night."

"Oh." She'd been fighting the same thoughts and didn't fault Margie for worrying.

Jill stilled. "What is it? Are *you* worried, too?"

She shrugged. "It's just that I haven't heard from him all week. Then with all the rumors on TV about some new album…it's hard not to think the worst."

Jill sat under the arbor on the bench. "I didn't realize. I thought the two of you were seeing each other. He's perfect for you. And correct me if I'm wrong, but he hits most of the markers on your list."

"Actually, he hits all of them. But I'm finally realizing that my stupid list doesn't mean anything. It's not going to guarantee the perfect man, because the perfect man doesn't exist."

"That's true. None of us is perfect. Do you love him?" Jill asked softly.

Kayla pressed her lips together and nodded. "Yes, I do, and it hurts so much that's he's not returning my calls. I don't know what's going on with him. The last time we spoke, everything seemed normal, at least normal for him. Then all of a sudden I see him on television and he stops communicating. I don't know what to do."

In the back of her mind she wondered if Derek's silence had something to do with Estelle, but she trusted him, even if Estelle could have been faking her newfound faith in the Lord, which was unlikely. Estelle might be a great actress, but her heart said the woman had changed. Estelle couldn't be the reason for Derek's silence. However, the alternatives hurt even worse—either he was no longer interested in *her*, or he was really returning to his old life.

Jill stood and picked her way to the edge of the float, then jumped off. "I want to pray with you." Jill grasped her hand. "Lord, I thank You for my friend and for caring so much for us. You understand our hurts and fears and that is so reassuring. Kayla needs Your guidance. She loves You, and she loves Derek. Please show her Your will and give her Your peace. Amen."

Kayla swallowed the lump in her throat. She always got emotional when someone prayed for her. Her stomach was such a jumble of nerves that she almost felt ill. "Thanks. Are we almost done yet?"

"Help will be here any minute. How about you bring in the rest of the supplies, then call it a night?"

"Are you sure?" Kayla hated leaving her friend with all this work, even if she had help on the way.

"Positive. I'm all rested up from my vacation and you've been towing the load all by yourself. Take the rest of the night for yourself." Jill looked intently at her. "Are you going to be okay?"

Kayla nodded. Honestly, she was more of a mess now than before. Going home and burying her head in her pillow was all she wanted to do. "I'll bring everything in and then see you bright and early tomorrow. Charlie has the parade under control, right?"

"Yes. We only need to worry about our grand reopening."

"Good." At least that was all Jill needed to worry about. Kayla, on the other hand, had more worries than she could handle.

Fifteen minutes later Kayla jogged to her car and started it up. Chilled, she turned the heater to high and headed home. She passed several cars coming up the driveway as she was headed out, which made her feel better about leaving.

Her characteristics-of-a-good-man list kept running through her mind. She'd created it to keep from getting hurt, but it hadn't helped. In fact, she'd trusted that thing with more faith than she'd given anyone or anything.

Where had God been in all of this? Why hadn't He stopped her or told her she was treating that list like an idol? She shuddered. Maybe He had, and she hadn't listened. The list had become her safety net, and the Lord had been squeezed out by her obsession. She'd placed her faith in the wrong source.

Tears clogged her throat as the full impact of her life choices hit her. Somewhere along the way she'd stopped depending on the Lord. "I'm so sorry. Please forgive me."

She pulled into her driveway and parked. A dim light glowed behind the curtains. Her mom must be home. She composed herself before going inside. A fire burned in the fireplace and her mom sat on the couch. Her eyelids drooped, and a book lay across her stomach.

"Hey, Mom," she said softly.

Mom's eyelids fluttered open. "Hi, honey." She yawned and stretched. "I'm beat. Think I'll head to bed."

"Sleep well." Kayla grabbed a few cushions and plopped down in front of the crackling flames, staring into the fire. A sudden desire to burn the list hit her and she couldn't shake the idea.

But the list was so much a part of her daily life it hung framed in her bedroom. No, hanging on to that list would be a mistake. She needed to let it go and put her trust completely in the Lord.

The fire crackled and snapped, drawing her attention. It had been ages since they'd built a fire. This couldn't be a coincidence; clearly God had a plan and was in control, as Helen pointed out earlier. She stood and went directly to her bedroom. The framed list hung beside a full-length mirror. She reached up and removed it from the wall. Flipping the frame over, she pried the backing off, then pulled out the aged sheet of paper penned in her teen years.

It hit her then how ridiculous holding on to this was. She marched out to the fireplace, wadded the notebook paper into a ball and tossed it into the flames. Within seconds the fire consumed the paper and with it years of misplaced hope.

Her hope was in the Lord and she would trust *Him* with her future—a future she hoped included Derek, but if it didn't, she'd trust the Lord regardless.

She sat there until the fire turned to coals, then went to bed. Tomorrow would be here all too soon.

Derek sat on a private jet gazing out the window. A glance at his watch made him cringe. His concert would start in an hour, and in all likelihood he wouldn't be there. To make things worse, he had no way of contacting Kayla. He'd tried before takeoff, but her phone had gone straight to voice mail. He didn't have the heart to tell her in a message what he had to say, so he'd hung up. Now that decision ate at him.

Would she ever be able to forgive him? He'd finally listened to all her messages and how her tone had changed over the course of the past week. By the last one, confusion and hurt filled her voice—he'd caused that and it turned his stomach.

At least his business in California was finished. Jerry had been arrested on multiple charges ranging from blackmail to human trafficking. He'd used his business as a celebrity manager as a front for his underworld dealings. He'd lost most of his clients and started to panic, afraid that if anyone else left, he wouldn't be able to continue hiding his illegal activities behind the cloak of his legitimate business.

When Derek had found out earlier today what had been going on, he'd been shocked. He rarely saw his manager in person and over the past year he'd had less and less contact with Jerry, which explained why he hadn't known, but still he felt as if he should have at least sensed that something was off with the man.

He shook his head. As frustrated as he'd been with the FBI, they had done a great job investigating and subsequently taking out a multistate human-trafficking ring in a coordinated effort earlier today. Jerry was in it up to his eyeballs, and he would spend a long time behind bars. Knowing that helped make up for everything, but he dreaded facing everyone in Oak Knoll. They would *not* be happy with him. He stared out the window and noted a familiar landmark. His pulse accelerated.

Chapter 19

Margie tapped her foot and waved her arms around. Kayla stood behind the counter at Flowers and More tuning out the woman's rant. Derek was a no-show for the sold-out concert.

"Well?" Margie stood with hands on her hips and a frown on her face.

"Well, what?"

"I asked if you'd go onstage and explain to the crowd why DJ Parker is a no-show."

"Me?" Kayla's voice rose a notch. "The concert is your baby."

"But the man is yours." She glared.

"He's not my man. I wish people would stop making assumptions."

Margie harrumphed.

"Fine. I'll do it." Kayla's heart pounded in her chest at the idea of an angry mob. People had bought tickets from as far away as Seattle. "I hope we don't have a riot."

"Just pour on that pageant charm and you'll have them begging *you* to sing." Margie waved. "I'm out of here."

Kayla's heart dropped. "Aren't you going to come with me?"

"Not a chance! Good luck." She fled the store, leaving Kayla to ponder her words.

What if *she* sang? She could sing their duet. Sure, it wouldn't be the same, but she could carry a tune well. Maybe if *someone* sang, the crowd wouldn't turn violent. Or maybe they'd throw food at her and chase her from the stage.

Either way, she'd said she'd deal with the announcement. Her palms sweated as she headed to the workroom. "Ah, Jill. I have to go."

Jill looked up from an arrangement she was working on and stilled. "What's wrong? You are white as a lily."

"Derek isn't here, and the concert is set to start in thirty minutes. I've been tasked with delivering the bad news to the crowd."

"Oh no. You can't go out there alone."

"I have to. I told Margie I would. Besides, I thought I might be able to appease them with a few DJ Parker songs."

"Sweetie, they are going to shred you. Those aren't just locals out there waiting in the hot sun. Half of that crowd doesn't know you or care who you are."

"Then you better have nine-one-one on speed dial, because I'm doing it."

"Oh, boy. I'm coming, too." Jill grabbed her keys.

"We need to hurry. I still have to go to Derek's studio and get his equipment."

"No, you don't. Charlie took care of all of that. They needed to do a sound check this morning, so Charlie stood in for Derek."

Kayla paused with her hand on the door. "For real? I had no idea. How'd he know to do that?"

"Beats me, but Charlie is a man of many talents. I have no idea why he's working for us other than to be with me." Jill shot her a cheeky grin.

"Okay, then, let's go. We may as well walk, because we won't be able to find close-up parking."

Jill pulled the front door shut. "Is that what you're wearing?"

Kayla looked down at the jeans and white sleeveless top she wore. "What's wrong with it? I was supposed to sing a duet with Derek and planned to wear this." She pulled Jill along beside her as they wove through clusters of people enjoying the festivities.

Jill panted. "Yeah, but that's when you were only singing a duet. I think something flashier would be better."

Kayla gave her friend an annoyed look. "You're not helping my confidence at all."

"Sorry." Jill pressed her lips together.

They turned onto the block with the park, and Kayla gasped. "Oh my goodness. I'm in big trouble." The hillside surrounding the stage was a sea of people both young and old. "I've never seen this many people in town before." She was not equipped to deal with this. Her pace slowed. *Lord, I can't do this without You. Please help!*

Jill patted her arm. "It's going to be fine," she said in a motherly tone.

"Easy for you to say," she mumbled. "Come on. We need to work our way around to the back side of the stage." Five minutes later they spotted Charlie and he waved them through security.

"Please tell me Derek is on his way? His note in the instructions he overnight-mailed to me said he thought he'd make it, but it would be close." Charlie looked from Jill to Kayla.

"He did?" Kayla wrung her hands. "Pray." She moved to stage left and stood in the wing while running through a few vocal exercises to warm her voice. She took several deep breaths in an attempt to calm her racing heart.

Voices chanted "DJ, DJ, DJ" over and over. She poked her head out just enough to see the crowd standing and clapping to the beat of their chant. Jill and Charlie moved up beside her.

Jill took her hand and squeezed. "We won't leave you. We'll be right here."

"Thanks." Kayla squared her shoulders as a sound technician slipped a microphone around her ear and adjusted the placement.

He covered the mouthpiece. "It's hot."

She nodded, then strutted onto the stage wearing her most confident smile. "Hey, everyone! How's it going?"

The chanting stopped, and the crowd erupted in applause.

"It seems DJ Parker has been delayed, so I'm hoping you will allow me to step in."

"We want DJ!" some woman shouted.

Kayla pushed down rising panic. Sweat trickled on her forehead. "Me, too, lady."

The crowd laughed. Kayla moved to the keyboard and struck a chord. "DJ and I worked on this together. It sounds better with him, but I hope you'll enjoy it. I know I do." She played the delicate intro to the ballad. The crowd quieted and a hush hovered over the park. She started into his verse, then noted a commotion in the crowd. They hated her. She hit a wrong note, and her voice cracked.

Suddenly a rich baritone joined her. She whipped her head to the side. Derek strolled onto the stage wearing dark-wash jeans. His acoustic guitar hung from his shoulder. He stopped center stage, plugged his guitar into the amp, then adjusted the instrument and seamlessly joined her.

When the song ended, the audience erupted into applause. "Give it up for Oak Knoll's very own Kayla Russell!" Derek strode to stand directly in front of her, then placed a hand over each of their mikes. "Thank you. I'm sorry you had to come out here alone."

Kayla's knees weakened, but her insides were bubbling with happiness. He'd come back! "It's okay. I'm glad you're here."

He winked. "Me, too. You mind accompanying on keyboard for the rest of the concert?"

"Happy to."

He got close to her ear and spoke quietly. "Charlie has all the music lined up the way I'm performing. I wasn't allowed to call, but it occurred to me last night no one ever said I couldn't send something by snail mail."

"You couldn't call?"

"Long story, but right now we have a concert to do." He removed his hand from their microphones. Strumming his guitar strings, he sat center stage on a stool and crooned out melody after melody. "This next song is one I wrote for a very special lady who once shared with me why she doesn't like Valentine's Day."

Kayla blinked and searched through the music. There was nothing there. Wait, what had he just said?

Derek faced the side of the stage she was on and chuckled. "You won't find any music for this song, Kayla. This one's for you. 'Valentine's Day 3-6-5.'"

"Until I met you, I didn't have a clue, No, I didn't have a clue about love.

Be my valentine—three-six-five.
E-ver-y day of the year.
Be my valentine—three-six-five.
Celebrate all through the year.
My valentine, oh, my valentine
Three hundred sixty-five days of the year."

Kayla's gaze locked on Derek as the song flowed from his lips. Her stomach flip-flopped when he shot her a dashing smile as the song ended. She stood and clapped.

Whistles pierced the air as the audience leaped to their feet and applauded.

Derek waved and bowed. He spotted Kayla drifting to the side of the stage and ran to her. "Kayla?" Had he blown it with the song? Maybe it was too much. "Are you okay?"

She turned to him with shining eyes. "I'm perfect. I loved the song."

They were out of view of the audience. He gently removed her microphone and then his own and passed them off to a sound guy. "I'm glad you liked it. I meant those words. I want every day for us to be like Valentine's Day. I don't want to express my love for you only one day a year."

Her grin widened. "You love me?"

"Duh." He playfully rolled his eyes and pulled her close. "Kayla Russell, all I've wanted since I left for LA was to see Jerry locked up and get home to you."

"Home. I like the sound of that."

"Me, too." He lowered his head and claimed her lips.

A dreamy look lit her eyes when she opened them. "I love you, too."

"I'm glad, but what about your list? Do I pass muster?" He raised a brow.

"I burned that silly thing. God showed me that I had

placed my trust in the list rather than in Him." A half smile touched her lips. "But for the record, you passed with straight A's."

He leaned forward until their foreheads met. "I didn't realize it was a graded thing."

She shrugged and pulled away slightly. "What happened to you? I've been trying to call all week. I all but gave up on you, until I got here and saw that you had everything under control. Charlie said you'd be here, or at least you were going to try, so I figured you had to have a plan."

"I had a plan, all right, but it didn't turn out at all like I expected. I thought I'd be an hour late, but the plane the FBI sent me home on was fast, and I mean fast. It helped that the plane could land at the airport in Salem. It was only a short drive from there."

"Good. Because I don't know what would've happened if you hadn't shown up when you did."

"They would have fallen in love with you just like me." He claimed her soft lips and drew her close. This was exactly how he wanted to spend the rest of his life.

Epilogue

One year later

Kayla leaned back in the gondola and listened as her husband sang a song to her in Italian. Their gondola glided along the canal in Venice, Italy, where they were spending their two-week honeymoon.

She thought back over the past year and what a whirlwind it had been. First her mother's elopement in Las Vegas, which had turned out to be an even bigger surprise than she'd expected because Jill and Charlie had decided to follow Kayla's mom's lead and elope as well in Las Vegas—one wedding right after the other.

Kayla fondly remembered her church wedding in their hometown seven months ago. Mom and Stan had come home. The biggest surprise guest, though, was Estelle Rogers, who told them she'd retired from showbiz and was opening a restaurant.

If anyone had told her a year ago that she'd be married

to the man of her dreams and that she'd be riding in a gondola in Italy while he serenaded her, she'd have laughed. Now all she could muster was a sappy smile.

It was nice to have Derek all to herself after having been on his farewell tour with him for the past six months. He'd signed the record contract with the stipulation he'd have to do only one tour and then he was done with the business. Her man was officially retired, and he was looking forward to returning to his old position as the music pastor.

"What's that grin for?" Derek tucked her close to his side.

"Just reminiscing. We've had a pretty amazing beginning to our life together."

"That's an understatement." He tilted his head and whispered, "Did I tell you today how much I love you?"

"Only a half dozen times." She caressed his face. "I love you, too."

He claimed her lips, and she melted in his arms.

Love was good. Very good indeed.

* * * * *